"Are you in town for long, ma'am?" Brett's voice drew her attention.

No. I'm leaving as soon as I drop Davy off at home."

"That's a shame."

Why? Because he wouldn't have an opportunity to weave his charming wiles around another susceptible female heart?

Abby glanced again toward her nephew, who was still talking with Trey. *Come on, Davy, let's go.*

Brett motioned in their direction. "A bright boy, that one, and he has a natural way with horses. You may have an accomplished horseman in the family one of these days."

"He wants a horse. Bad." She smiled inwardly at the remembrance of her own childhood demands.

"Is your brother harboring any other pretty sisters?" Brett quirked a smile. "I may have to talk with him about holding out on friends."

He's a flirt. The women warned you. Don't take his flattery to heart. Nevertheless, her breath came more quickly at the approving sparkle in his eyes.

Books by Glynna Kaye

Love Inspired

Dreaming of Home
Second Chance Courtship
At Home in His Heart
High Country Hearts
Look-Alike Lawman
A Canyon Springs Courtship
Pine Country Cowboy

GLYNNA KAYE

treasures memories of growing up in small Midwestern towns—in Iowa, Missouri, Illinois—and vacations spent in another rural community with the Texan side of the family. She traces her love of storytelling to the many times a houseful of great-aunts and great-uncles gathered with her grandma to share hours of what they called "windjammers"—candid, heartwarming, poignant and often humorous tales of their youth and young adulthood.

Glynna now lives in Arizona, and when she isn't writing she's gardening and enjoying photography and the great outdoors.

Pine Country Cowboy
Glynna Kaye

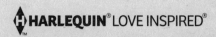

HARLEQUIN® LOVE INSPIRED®

Recycling programs
for this product may
not exist in your area.

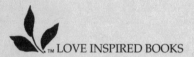

™ LOVE INSPIRED BOOKS

ISBN-13: 978-0-373-87881-9

PINE COUNTRY COWBOY

www.Harlequin.com

Printed in U.S.A.

The Lord is close to the brokenhearted
and saves those who are crushed in spirit.
—*Psalms* 34:18

Forget the former things; do not dwell on the past.
See, I am doing a new thing! Now it springs up;
do you not perceive it? I am making a way
in the desert and streams in a wasteland.
—*Isaiah* 43:18–19

To Uncle Ron and Aunt Kay…and in memory of my cousin Teri, who inspired those whose lives she touched as she courageously battled cystic fibrosis.

Chapter One

The last thing Abby Diaz needed was to be surrounded by little kids and pestered by a flirtatious cowboy.

At the moment, she had the misfortune of both.

She sucked in a steadying breath, acutely aware of the echoing chirp of sparrows in the indoor arena's rafters, the smell of straw, hay and horses—and the engaging smile of the good-looking man patiently awaiting a response to his question.

At least she wouldn't be in Canyon Springs much longer. In a few hours she'd be sailing her Chevy down the curving mountain road to Phoenix, then pushing farther southward through the desert to Tucson and home. It had been foolish to make the trip anyway, a futile, final grasping by her rapidly ebbing faith.

"So what do you say, pretty lady?" the sandy-haired cowboy with impossibly wide shoulders urged again, his low, mellow voice teasing her ears. Dressed in boots, faded jeans and a Western-cut shirt, he tipped back his summer straw hat as twinkling hazel eyes studied her with unconcealed interest. "It will take half a minute to lead another horse out here and get your lessons started right along with these kids."

Was he out of his mind? "I'll pass, thank you."

He briefly dipped his head in acknowledgment, a smile twitching at his lips. Then he glanced at the half dozen grade-schoolers milling around them, including her brother Joe's son. Since entering the arena, Davy had stuck glue-like to her side despite only having met her three days ago.

The seven-year-old had been excited about coming today, begging his almost-nine-months pregnant step-mother not to renege on his first riding lesson. But after another sleepless night of acute discomfort, Meg hadn't been up to it. With his daddy working an extended shift as a regional paramedic and Grandpa Diaz seeing to an RV park crisis, Aunt Abby had been dragged into this family-oriented outing. She'd planned to drop Davy off and return for him later, but on the drive to the High Country Equine Center—which most locals still called Duffy's after the original owner—the brown-eyed boy seemed to be having second thoughts about the adventure. She'd hung around for moral support.

Avoiding the cowboy's assessing gaze, Abby rested her hand on her nephew's shoulder and gave it a reassuring pat. "This will be fun, Davy—won't it, Gina?"

His best buddy, a blonde pigtailed dynamo, nodded emphatically, her instructor-issued riding helmet bobbing atop her head. "Majorly fun."

Not to be outdone by a girl, Davy shook off his aunt's hand and gave a manly nod reminiscent of his father. "That's right. Majorly fun." He cut a glance upward. "You don't have to stay if you don't want to, Aunt Abby."

That caught the cowboy's attention. "Aunt Abby?"

"Daddy's little sister," Davy announced proudly, stuffing his hands into the back pockets of his jeans.

"Well, what do you know?" The man's smile broadened as he again caught her eye. "Joe has a sister? Where's he been hiding you, ma'am?"

Obviously this man, no more than a handful of years

older than her, wasn't a Canyon Springs native or he'd know the whole story. But there was no point in enlightening a stranger on the Diaz family history.

"He didn't hide her," Davy piped up with a giggle. "Aunt Abby lives in Tucson. She's a librarian."

"Davy," Abby said firmly before the boy could further elaborate on her personal affairs. She didn't want him sharing with the world that she'd recently lost her librarian position and not too many months before that had sent her fiancé packing. Or at least the latter was what she'd allowed her family to assume.

Today—the first of June—was to have been her wedding day.

"A librarian," the cowboy echoed, his gaze flicking over her appreciatively. If the sparkle in his eyes was any indication, for a reason known only to him he found that bit of information amusing.

He held out his gloved hand. "Good to meet you, Aunt Abby. Diaz, is it?"

She nodded and reluctantly shook his hand.

"I'm Brett Marden."

A shrill whistle pierced the air.

"Brett! Let's go!" Another cowboy-hatted man, this one taller and walking with a slight limp, made his way across the arena's expanse. He clapped his hands and motioned to the portable corral assembled on the far side of the arena where half a dozen saddled quarter horses waited quietly.

Abby had met Trey Kenton, manager of the equine facility, her first night back in town and remembered his wife, Kara, from grade school. It had come as a shock to discover she and the other woman might be stepsisters in the not-too-distant future. *Thanks for the warning, Dad.*

Brett studied Abby a moment longer. "Why don't you stick around, Aunt Abby? You never can tell… Could be you'll find something that catches your interest."

He stepped back with what she instinctively knew was a well-practiced wink.

Warmth crept into her face. Did he mean *him?* Of all the...

Not waiting for a response, he lightly rapped his knuckles on her nephew's helmeted head, then spread his arms wide to herd the youngsters toward the corral. "No running, no yelling. We have things we need to go over before you get to ride."

Abby stared after him. Find something that catches your interest, indeed. Talk about an over-the-top ego. Nevertheless, her gaze lingered on the masculine form as he crossed the arena, a booted Pied Piper with a covey of trailing kids attempting to mimic his confident stride.

"You may as well come on over here and have a seat," a feminine voice called from somewhere behind her. "Abby, is it?"

Jerked from her reverie, Abby turned toward a small semicircle of folding chairs placed just inside one of the arena's side gates. She hadn't noticed the arrangement when she and Davy had slipped inside to join the other kids. Apparently Brett Marden had been a bit too distracting. Four women now claimed the seating area—a grayhaired lady and three others near Abby's late twenties or slightly younger. One, the spokesperson she assumed, patted the sole empty chair next to her in invitation.

A knot tightened in Abby's stomach. Why'd the most friendly one have to be holding a baby?

"Yes, Abby. Abby Diaz." With considerable effort she returned the smiles of the women. Then she reluctantly closed the distance between them to take the seat next to the woman who cuddled her napping infant close. If they'd caught her name, they'd probably heard the whole conversation between her and the flirtatious cowboy.

"I'm Davy's aunt," she nevertheless confirmed. "From Tucson."

"Joey's sister." The familiar-looking older woman on the far side of the semicircle nodded knowingly. Abby sensed she was aware of the family's sordid history, how Abby's parents divorced when she was ten, with her mother taking both her and middle child Ed and leaving teenage Joe to be raised by their father.

"Are you visiting, Abby?" the woman continued with an encouraging smile. "Or have you come home?"

Even though she'd once lived here for a decade, it had been more than strange to drive through Canyon Springs a few days ago for the first time since childhood. To pass down Main Street and by the elementary school. To eat lunch at Kit's Lodge. To again spend the night under her father's roof at his Lazy D Campground and RV Park. It was surprising how much she remembered and how little had changed. But home? Not even close.

"I'm visiting my family for a few days."

The woman to the left of Abby leaned forward and she caught the faint scent of baby powder and a glimpse of a pretty, rounded face in the blanketed bundle in her arms.

"How *is* Meg?" the brown-haired woman whispered.

The other three women nodded at her words, concern darkening their eyes.

"She's hanging in there." Abby didn't know how well these four knew Meg and Joe, so she wasn't about to elaborate on the family's whispered concerns for Meg's health. "She's looking forward to being a few pounds lighter."

The women laughed and Abby's tension eased. She could get through this.

"I'm Mina Ricks, here with my boy," the woman next to her offered before glancing down with a proud smile at the infant in her arms. "And this is Ruthy."

Then she motioned to each of the women, starting with

the blonde seated on the other side of Abby. "This is Melody Smith, who brought a neighbor's daughter today. Joy Haines is here with her twins. And Janet Logan accompanied her grandson."

Memory clicked and Abby again focused her attention on the woman who'd asked if she'd come home. "Mrs. Logan. You ran the school library and were my Sunday school teacher, too."

A sturdy, outdoorsy, take-charge kind of woman who didn't fit any of the librarian stereotypes Abby was all too familiar with, she'd seemed as old as the hills when Abby had been in grade school. But in reality she was probably even now only in her early to mid-sixties.

"Call me Janet. I'm still the librarian and a Sunday school teacher." The woman's gaze warmed. "I wondered if you'd remember me. It's been such a long time. But my goodness, how you remind me of your beautiful mother."

"Thank you." The compliment was well intended, but she wasn't fooled. In reality she didn't come close to her mother's striking looks or her vivacious personality.

"Do you remember me, too?"

Abby turned to the young woman next to her who was looking at her hopefully.

Melody. Melody. She hated this. Everyone knew who she was, but she'd been put on the spot so many times over the past few days that she'd become paranoid about meeting people. That was one more reason to get out of town. She hoped this woman about her age wasn't another cousin. The whole town seemed to be crawling with them.

"I wasn't a Smith back then. Or a blonde." Melody brushed back her layered golden tresses. "You might remember me as the chubby carrot-haired girl who tried to crawl out the second-grade-classroom window—and got stuck."

Abby's eyes widened with belated recognition. What a fuss that incident had created. "Oh, *that* Melody!"

"I've slimmed down considerably...." The young woman laughed as she spread her fingers wide to protectively cradle a barely rounded abdomen, and Abby tensed, sensing what was coming next. "But I understand that won't last much longer. I'm due in November. Our first."

"Congratulations." Abby swallowed the knot in her throat. "That's wonderful."

The others joined in with cheerful words of encouragement, an exclusive little club of women who'd been there, done that, who reveled in the blessings and agonies of childbearing and motherhood.

Grasping for a diversion, Abby turned toward the corral where Brett and Trey instructed the kids on horse safety. Trey was a handsome man, but it was the self-assured Brett who now held her attention. Brett, with the broad shoulders, dimpled grin and laugh lines crinkling around his eyes. In spite of his unapologetically flirtatious behavior, her heart beat faster.

"Don't pay any mind to Brett," freckle-faced Joy commented almost as if following Abby's train of thought. "He can't help but turn on the charm when he's around a female."

Melody laughed. "A born sweet-talker if there ever was one."

So Abby had pegged him right. A superficial skirt chaser.

"Don't be too hard on that young man," Mrs. Logan— Janet—chided gently. "He's got a heart of gold."

"He's been in Canyon Springs about a year and a half and everyone seems to love him. Hard not to." Mina shifted the sleeping baby in her arms. "But my advice, Abby? If you're looking for a keeper, steer clear. I'm not sure even a lasso and piggin' string could keep that one corralled."

Joy laughed, then Melody chimed in. "But let it be said that Britney Bennett isn't one to take no for an answer."

"Isn't that the truth. Poor Brett."

Janet smiled, shaking her head.

Little towns. Abby had just met these women and already they were sharing advice of the heart with a total stranger.

"Don't worry about me." Abby lifted her chin slightly, as if to assure them she wasn't the susceptible sort and could take care of herself. "I'm going back to Tucson today when Davy's finished with his lesson."

"So soon?" Janet's forehead puckered. "I was hoping you'd stay awhile and could be recruited to help at an upcoming summer camp for kids. You should at least stay for church tomorrow. I'm sure there are many others who'd love to see you all grown-up."

Abby forced a smile, again conscious of the empty, echoing rafters above, the tinny cheep of sparrows and a horse's whinny reverberating through the vast space. Reasons to make a getaway were rapidly multiplying. But she wouldn't admit to these kindhearted women that she hadn't been to church in five months. Not since the day doctors confirmed she'd forever remain childless—and her displeased fiancé had walked out the door.

From across the arena, Brett's gaze again roamed to Davy's aunt Abby. She was a pretty little filly with big brown eyes and below-the-shoulder, straight black hair demurely pulled back with a satin ribbon. Although dressed conservatively in dark gray slacks and a simple white blouse, that slim waist nevertheless invited a man to slip his arm around it and draw her close. But except for a glimpse of warmth directed at her nephew, he'd yet to see a smile and could only imagine how a laugh might transform her sadness-kissed features.

That there was a melancholy reflected in her eyes, in her bearing, he had no doubt. Did others notice or was he too finely attuned to the nuances of sorrow? He'd worn that heavy cloak himself, hadn't he? Sometimes it still weighed on him when he least expected it.

"When do we get to ride?" Abby's nephew demanded as Trey, the equine center's manager, expounded on safety precautions when working around horses.

The other kids nodded eagerly, including Janet Logan's grandson, Ace, and Brett grinned. Small for his age, the fair-haired fifth-grader had good coloring today and appeared to be breathing well. That wasn't always the case. He might not be up to every lesson this coming summer but, when it came to facing challenges head-on, the kid took after his grandma with a can-do attitude they could all learn from.

"We're almost to the riding part," Trey assured the children as he turned to his own saddled horse to demonstrate mounting and dismounting.

Today they'd let the kids ride in the corral, closely supervised, to allow them a taste of what they were here for. The next lessons would include vocabulary, equine anatomy and basics of horse and equipment care, as well as getting them started on the fundamentals of horsemanship.

Brett glanced again at Davy, several years younger than Brett's own son would now have been. Jeremy, who'd been held close in his father's arms for five hard but precious years…and was now held even more tenderly by his Heavenly Father.

Smiling down at the dark-haired boy, a deeply buried longing of his heart surfaced. Would he ever have another son? A daughter? Could he ever love another woman in such a way that she'd choose to commit to him for a lifetime and not shake her fist at God and walk out when the road became unbearably rocky?

He again looked over the tops of the children's heads toward the group of women seated near the gate. He'd glimpsed heartache in the eyes of Abby Diaz. With three sisters of his own, he never liked seeing a lady in distress and always did his best to cheer them up, to make things right. Maybe when they wrapped things up here he could have a few words with her. Tease out a smile. Maybe even coax a laugh.

"Hand over that little lady, Mina." Brett Marden tucked his gloves into his belt and reached for the now wide-awake infant. He paid no mind to Abby, for which she was grateful. The chattering, elementary-school-aged children still dawdled as they made their way across the arena toward the adults, but Brett had beelined to the group as soon as lessons concluded.

When the young mother released her baby to Brett's care, he cuddled the squirming bundle close, nuzzling her until she rewarded him with a squealing, toothless grin. "She's getting prettier every day, just like her mommy."

Mina gave Abby a "what did I tell you?" look, but nonetheless smiled up at Brett, basking in his generous praise.

"Everyone says she looks like her father," Mina corrected, and Brett pulled back with a frown to stare down into the little girl's eyes.

He shook his head. "I have to disagree, ma'am. Anyone who says that must be trying to get on the good side of her daddy. Everybody knows her old man's a big ugly brute."

The ladies laughed as he handed the child back to Mina. Then placing his hands firmly on his narrow, jeans-clad hips, he pinned Melody with a knowing gaze.

"Now, young lady, what's this I'm hearing around town about you and Kent having a bun in the oven?"

Melody's cheeks flushed crimson, her hand again self-consciously dropping to her abdomen, the snug knit top obviously designed to enhance the barest of baby bumps. "A few weeks before Thanksgiving."

Brett squinted one eye. "Boy or girl?"

"We don't want to know," she teased back with a saucy tilt to her head, obviously relishing being the focus of his good-natured attention. "We want him—or her—to be an old-fashioned surprise."

"Good plan." Brett nodded approval. "Congratulations, little mama."

He turned to Abby and winked as if fully aware she'd been watching him. Caught off guard, she looked away, searching for Davy, who still lingered at the corral with Trey, patting the nose of a chestnut horse.

Behind her, Brett reminded Janet he'd be in touch before his shift at Singing Rock Cabin Resort started tonight. So he worked for her aunt and uncle, too? Then as the ladies shooed their charges out the arena gate, Abby rose and slung her purse strap over her shoulder, uncomfortably aware of Brett's lingering gaze.

Didn't the man have anything better to do than to torment her? Okay, maybe *torment* was too strong a word. But it seemed clear he wasn't satisfied having the bevy of young mothers eating out of his hand. He needed assurance that the newcomer's adoration was secured, as well.

Don't hold your breath, cowboy.

She started off to get Davy, but less than half a dozen yards into her journey Brett joined her, his eyes still smiling almost as if holding on to an unshared secret.

"So Joe has a little sister."

Reluctantly, she drew to a halt. "That's me."

For a moment she thought he was going to say "Why didn't he ever mention you?" She couldn't take offense if he did. Family usually talked about family. But there would be no reason for her brother to mention her in casual conversation. Five years apart in age, they'd barely been in contact after Mom took off with her when Joe was fifteen. Nevertheless, her little-girl heart had missed him and he'd told her a few days ago that he'd missed her, too.

"Are you in town for long, ma'am?" Brett's voice drew her back to the present.

"No. I'm leaving as soon as I drop Davy off at home."

"That's a shame."

Why? Because he wouldn't have an opportunity to weave his charming wiles around another susceptible female heart?

She glanced again toward her nephew, who was still talking with Trey. *Come on, Davy, let's go.*

Brett motioned in their direction. "A bright boy, that one, and he has a natural way with horses. You may have an accomplished horseman in the family one of these days."

"He wants a horse. Bad." She smiled inwardly at the remembrance of her own childhood demands. What kid doesn't think they want a pony? "Joe thought it might be good to let him try it out. Kids often lose interest when they discover an imagined event, toy or pet isn't as advertised."

The cowboy nodded. "You can say the same thing of adults, I imagine."

Where was he coming from with that comment? But he sure nailed it on the head. The shallowness of commitment on the part of her fiancé had been nothing short of deplorable. "I guess so."

"Is your brother harboring any other pretty siblings?" Brett quirked a smile. "I may have to talk with him about holding out on friends."

He's a flirt. The women warned you. Don't take his flattery to heart. Nevertheless, her breath came more quickly at the approving sparkle in his eyes.

"There's one other…" She couldn't help but toy, noticing with gratification how a brow lifted in surprised interest. "But our brother, Ed, might take exception to being termed pretty."

Brett's amused gaze pinned her just as her cell phone vibrated silently in the purse resting against her hip. *Please don't let it be Gene again.* Since Sunday evening her ex-fiancé had been calling. Emailing. Texting. His messages were brief, only that he needed to talk to her. With each attempt to make contact, her hopes—and outrage—rose in unison.

Brett cocked his head to the side. "Is something wrong, ma'am?"

She wished he'd stop calling her that. It made her sound as old as dirt. "My phone's vibrating." She patted the purse at her side. "Incoming call."

"Don't mind me. Go ahead. Take it."

With a grimace of apology, she pulled out the phone. Not Gene, thank goodness, but her older brother, Davy's dad.

It was already nice getting more frequent calls from Joe. While they'd kept in contact sporadically through the years, they had a long way to go to rebond. Maybe they never fully would. But despite him not being around much the past few days, he *was* making an effort to reconnect, which was more than Dad seemed to be doing.

"Hey, Joe, what's up?"

"Meg's being air-vacced to the hospital at Show Low."

Her throat tightened at his flat tone, recognizing he'd shifted into paramedic mode. The levelheaded corpsman pattern from his navy days divorced emotion from the situation at hand, conveying that the air transport was more serious than Meg merely going into a much-anticipated labor.

"Is she—"

"I'm on my way there now. She says you have Davy."

Abby quickly confirmed the boy was still deep in conversation with Trey. "I do. He's right here."

"Can you keep him for a while? Stay with him at the house if we don't get back by tonight?"

"Maybe…" Dad could take care of Davy, couldn't he? Or Olivia, Joe and Abby's cousin who'd married Meg's brother? But no, Joe needed immediate assurance that things were under control on the home front. "Sure. No problem."

"Davy has a key."

"Okay."

"Thanks, sis. You're an answered prayer. I'll call you when I know more."

Heart still pounding, she gripped the phone as her gaze met Brett's troubled one. "Wait— Joe? Will Meg— Is the baby— Are they going to be okay?"

Chapter Two

Gut-punched at the implications of the one-sided conversation, Brett watched as Abby slipped the phone back into her purse with trembling fingers.

"The baby's on its way?"

"Maybe." Abby's dark eyes, wide with alarm, met his. "Meg's not due for two more weeks, but she's being air-vacced to Show Low. Joe will call again after he gets there and has more details."

"But he thinks she and the baby are going to be okay?" He'd heard her ask that question.

She bit gently down on her lower lip. "He doesn't know. He says to keep them in our prayers."

Brett gave a confirming nod, a prayer already pumping through his being along with the rush of adrenaline coursing through his veins. Babies. Moms. He knew what was at stake. "You can count on me."

Something in Abby's eyes flickered. Surprise? Doubt?

"Thank you." She drew in a deep breath and let it out slowly. "The baby... It's a girl. Jorelle. Jo. After her daddy, except without the *e*."

"I imagine everybody will be calling her Jori before she's even out of diapers."

"Jori. I like that." An ever-so-faint smile touched the

woman's lips, then she turned to watch as Davy and Trey headed in their direction, her nephew proudly leading Trey's horse, Taco. "I'd better round up Davy and get him back home."

"You'll be lucky if you can drag him out of here with a tractor. Looks like he and ol' Taco are buds now."

"It does, doesn't it?" She took a strengthening breath and he intuitively knew where her thoughts had headed—to what she'd tell Davy about his stepmother's situation.

He lightly touched her arm and, as she turned uncertainly toward him, he clearly read concern for her family in her eyes.

"Don't worry, ma'am. You'll be given the words to explain his mom's absence. To reassure him. He'll be fine."

She blinked rapidly, hugging her arms to herself in an almost protective gesture.

"But he hardly knows me. What if—" She compressed her lips together, her dark eyes challenging him for answers to questions she dared not utter. What if something was wrong with the baby? What if his mommy… What if she was all alone with Davy should she get such a call?

Stepping closer, he reached for her hand, holding it securely when she tried to draw it back. Warm, soft, fine-boned. "God will tell you what to say, what to do. But don't dwell on the negative. I don't know if there's any truth to it, but I've heard babies sometimes come early at higher elevations. Everything's going to be fine. You wait and see."

She stared into his eyes, absorbing his words, and his heart rate ramped up a notch. *Calm her, Lord. Let her feel Your presence. And while You're at it, You may need to give me the strength to let go of her hand.*

After a long moment, she gave a slight nod, the worst of the worry in her eyes subsiding. He gave her hand an encouraging squeeze.

"Aunt Abby! Look at me."

Abby immediately pulled her hand from his and the two again turned as Trey and the boy neared, a toothy grin spread across the youngster's face.

When they'd come to a halt in front of her, Abby gave a firm pat to the chestnut's neck, not timid about it as he would have expected.

She smiled. "You looked good out there, Davy."

"He did," Brett confirmed as the boy reluctantly handed over the reins to Trey, then removed his riding helmet and reached up to set it atop the saddle horn.

Brett whipped off his own hat and stepped up to place it on the dark-haired head. "Now you look like a real cowboy."

Davy beamed up at him.

"Get your daddy to buy you a hat."

"And some real boots, too?" With a roll of his eyes, Davy looked down at the indignity of his makeshift attire. The class required footwear with a heel so little feet couldn't slip through stirrups, but today Joe's son was making do with a pair of laced, heeled work boots. Yep, the boy needed himself a hat and a pair of genuine cowboy boots.

Brett clapped him on the shoulder. "Mention that to your daddy, too."

"Good job, Davy." Trey lifted a hand in farewell. "See you at church tomorrow."

Bubbling over with barely contained happiness, the boy returned Brett's hat, then turned to half walk, half skip his way across the arena floor. Abby watched him in thoughtful silence, then turned again to Brett.

"Thank you," she murmured almost shyly, and he again detected an underlying sadness in her eyes. She nodded to Trey and had barely turned away when a laughing Davy dashed back to grab her hand. Together they jogged toward the arena's exit.

Brett twirled his hat on his finger, unable to suppress a grin.

"I've seen a lot of things in my day," Trey said, shaking his head as he scratched Taco behind the ear. "But now I've seen it all. Nobody tops you, buddy. Ninety minutes into an introduction and you're already holding hands with Davy's aunt. What was that all about?"

Avoiding Trey's incredulous stare, Brett gripped the brim of his hat as he recalled the delicate softness of Abby's fingers cupped in his work-roughened hands. The sweet, clean smell of her up close and her raven hair shimmering, waiting to be loosed from its ribbon clasp.

A not-unexpected weight pressed in on his heart and he scuffed a boot in the dirt, shaking off the too-vivid memory. While they were nice to look at and fun to flirt with, he wasn't in the market for another lady in his life. A wife. It wasn't likely God would give him the go-ahead for such as that again, anyway. Besides, he needed to stay focused on helping Janet Logan revive that weeklong summer camp for disease-disabled kids. She was the sole person in Canyon Springs who knew why the project was close to his heart. He liked it that way, between the two of them and God.

"It was all about nothin', that's what," he said with a chuckle as he belatedly remembered Trey was waiting for an answer. "At least nothing like what you're thinking."

"Yeah, right."

Sobering, Brett cut a look at his friend and employer. "She got a call that Joe's wife's being rushed to the hospital in Show Low. She needed reassurance, that's all."

Trey smiled as the truth dawned. "The baby's coming?"

Brett squinted against the light coming in from the open doorway at the end of the building, watching a silhouetted Abby and her nephew heading out to their vehicle. She'd be telling him now. Telling him his mommy wouldn't be

"Hey, Meg has something she wants to talk to you about. Just a sec."

She eased herself down onto a kitchen chair, waiting as he handed the phone to his wife with a few murmured words. Heard a kiss. Must be nice to have a supportive spouse, one who stuck by you no matter what.

"Abby?"

Meg's usually perky voice was far less so today, and Abby envisioned the short-haired brunette, her face now much fuller than in her wedding pictures, stretched out in a hospital bed after the upset of the previous day.

"I hate to ask one more thing of you," her sister-in-law continued. "So I apologize in advance. I know you intended to go home yesterday."

"Never mind that." She plucked absently at a woven place mat. "What can I do for you?"

"Until a few minutes ago, I'd forgotten the kindergarten Sunday school teacher is out of town this weekend. I'm her assistant. Her backup. Would you fill in for me this morning?"

That meant a room full of little kids, probably next door to the nursery. She'd be facing another battery of "do you remember me?" people, too. But how could she say no?

"I've prepared the lesson," Meg rushed on. "The activities, too. Everything's in the wicker trunk in the living room."

"How many kids are we talking about?" Although she'd long dreamed of one of her own, Abby hadn't much interaction with the younger set. Brother Ed had no children and Joe's son, Davy, by his now-deceased first wife had grown up in San Diego, where she'd had no in-person contact with him until now.

"Usually four kids, maybe five. But this time of year, with the tourist season beginning, we plan for eight, then up to twelve once school is out and the season is in full swing."

Potentially eight kids. "Ohhh…kay."

"You don't sound like it's okay."

Abby glanced down at her jeans and tank top. Not exactly grubbies, but hardly churchwear. She'd have to change. "I'm reconfiguring the morning in my mind. Davy and I aren't quite ready to dash out the door."

"Sometimes you have to light a fire under him to get him moving."

"Oh, he's up and had breakfast. We've run into a slight delay." She hoped the yellow Lab hadn't chewed up the shoe beyond repair. "Don't worry about the class. I'll have it covered."

"Thanks, Abby. I feel bad asking people to step in at the last minute. I had to call the school district to tell them I'll miss these final days of the semester."

From the dismal tone of her voice, disappointment weighed heavily on the high school science teacher. It was obvious even from their brief acquaintance that she loved teaching and her students.

"Joe says you might be released this afternoon, so get plenty of rest. You and Jori—" she tried out the nickname on her tongue, still liking the sound of it "—need all your strength for the final big event."

"Jori?"

"That's what one of Davy's riding instructors, Brett Marden, is calling her."

"So you met Brett, did you?" A lilt of amusement colored Meg's innocent question.

The image of Brett's dancing eyes and flash of even white teeth returned with a rush. His "could be you'll find something that catches your interest" comment echoed in her ears as she rubbed her palm down the side of her jeans, recalling yesterday's surprisingly gentle touch when he'd unexpectedly taken her hand in his. "We spoke for a few minutes."

"What do you think of him?"

She stood and moved to stand at the French door leading to the patio, focusing on the beautiful morning in an attempt to force out lingering images of her nephew's riding instructor.

"He's nice. Davy seems to like him."

Meg snorted. "You're holding back on me. How about the part that he's gorgeous, has a killer smile and can charm the hair right off your head?"

"I guess I wasn't paying that much attention." Would lightning strike her for the denial?

Her sister-in-law's laughter pealed through the phone. "It sounds as if we need to get your eyes checked. He has so many female hearts wrapped around his little finger it's not even funny. So be on your toes, girl, if you run into him again."

She wouldn't be running into him again if she had anything to say about it. There was something unsettling about the man, something that set her senses on high alert with red flashing lights. Caution. Warning. Do not enter.

"You forget, Meg." Abby shoved away thoughts of the too-friendly cowboy. "I've come out of a relationship that didn't end in a happily ever after. I'm in no hurry to walk that path again."

"I'm sorry. I forgot."

Hearing the sincere regret in Meg's voice, Abby wished she hadn't said anything. She didn't want anyone's sympathy. Not about any of it, which is why she'd kept the truth behind Gene's departure from her family and had allowed them to assume she'd broken off the relationship as she'd done others in the past. No one anticipating the celebration of a new arrival needed the downer of her childless reality intruding into their midst.

"That's okay. I'm fine. I'm not looking for a replacement anytime soon." Abby turned away from the pine-studded view to pace the kitchen floor. "So forget about me and concentrate on your new arrival. You're going to have that baby before you know it."

Meg sighed. "I hope so. I know God has it all under control, but yesterday I was so scared. I still am even though I'm trying not to be."

Abby halted. It seemed strange for Meg to confide in her, an almost stranger. She must be searching for reassurance wherever she could get it. Would they have been friends by now had Abby not eschewed her brother's wedding last year? Her relationship with Gene had been off to a promising start and he'd invited her to meet his Seattle-based parents during spring break—which happened to coincide with Joe and Meg's wedding date. With hardly a second thought, she'd eagerly joined Gene. Bad choice on her part, in retrospect.

"I want my little girl to be healthy and happy," the voice over the phone murmured softly.

"She will be, Meg. Everything's going to be fine." Would it? That's what Brett said and, for some crazy reason, she'd believed him. He'd seemed so certain and had promised to pray. Abby had been praying, too, but felt like a hypocrite asking favors for someone when she'd seen prayers for herself come to nothing. "Take a deep breath and don't worry about anything here. Davy and I will be on our way to church shortly."

Just as soon as she got that shoe away from the pup.

Chapter Three

"Hey, who's the gal with Davy Diaz?"

Jake Talford, standing outside the front door of Canyon Springs Christian Church, nodded toward the education wing of the building.

Brett turned to take a look and his spirits inexplicably took flight. As always, he felt a sense of anticipation as he approached the native stone building nestled among tall-trunked ponderosa pine trees, its bell tower topped by a cross. But today that expectancy was heightened by the sight of Abby ushering her nephew toward a side door. So she hadn't gone home yesterday after all.

Abby was dressed in a black skirt, burgundy V-neck top and what his sisters called espadrilles, with her hair fastened behind her head in a schoolmarmish bun. Despite her reserved manner, the look didn't suit her.

He watched until the pair disappeared inside, then turned back to his friend. "That's Abby Diaz. Joe's sister."

The city councilman raised a brow. "You're kidding. I didn't know he had a sister."

"Welcome to the club." At least he wasn't the lone person Joe hadn't confided in.

They chatted for several more minutes about the promising Arizona Diamondbacks season and Jake and his fiancée's wedding plans. But Brett had a hard time concentrating on the conversation. If Abby was at church with Davy, did that mean Meg had safely delivered the baby—or not?

As an older couple approached the doorway where the two men stood, he stepped back and gave Jake a parting nod. "See you later."

He jogged down the covered walkway to the education wing door, whipped off his hat and entered. What was Davy now? A first-grader until school let out for the summer? Abby would likely have been taking him to his classroom, then maybe joining one of the adult classes as he, too, intended to do.

He peeked in the interior window of the first grade class and spied Davy pulling out a chair at the table. Brett opened the door with an apologetic smile at the teacher and whispered to Abby's nephew. "Davy, where's your aunt?"

The boy looked up and smiled a greeting. "She's teaching kindergarten for Mommy."

His heart hitched. Kindergarten. Roughly the same age as Jeremy when he'd held him in his arms those final hours and kissed him goodbye.

Squaring his shoulders, he nodded his thanks, then shut the door. At the next classroom he looked through the window. Sure enough, a bewildered-looking Abby stood in the midst of half a dozen or so little kids, the noise level rising with every passing second even with the classroom door closed. Unsmiling, she appeared to be pleading with her charges to settle down, but the kids didn't pay her any attention.

This looked to be a rescue operation.

He opened the door and slipped inside. Then he shut it behind him, tossed his hat to the top of a supply cabinet and squatted to kid level, savoring the memorable scent of glue sticks and crayons. It took two seconds for the majority of the children to come running. The remaining two, probably summer visitors, hung back, watchful.

The local kids crowded in close.

"Hi, Brett! Can I wear your hat?"

"Are you going to teach our Sunday school class?"

"Did you ride your horse to church?"

"Where's Elmo?"

Laughing, he glanced up at Abby, who didn't look happy at the interruption. Couldn't she see he'd come to her aid? He gave each child a hug, then shook the hands of the new kids, solemnly introducing himself and asking their names.

"Brett is awesome," Betsy Davis, motherlike, assured the visitors. "We love him."

"Yeah." A ponytailed Mary Kenton, the pastor's oldest daughter, gave him another hug.

The others joined in with a cacophony of affirmations and the noise level escalated again. Conscious of the nursery across the hall and the adjoining first grade classroom, Brett stood and placed his finger to his lips. "I think it's time to play—"

"I do have a lesson prepared." Abby lifted a teacher's guide in protest as if suspecting he intended to hijack the sharing of God's word for an hour of recreational pursuits.

"Little red schoolhouse!" the local kids shouted in unison, guessing the game Brett had been about to suggest. Giggling, they hurried to be seated around a low, rectangular table.

He shrugged as he shot Abby a grin that she didn't return.

"This is so cool," Betsy informed the visitors as the chatter continued around the table. "His mom taught him this game."

"And her mom taught it to her," Brett added. Grandma was a sly one. As a youngster, he'd fallen for it for years.

Glancing at an obviously disapproving Abby, he merely waved her toward one of the diminutive chairs. "Come on, ma'am, you won't want to miss this."

With a crease still etching her forehead, she pulled out a chair and carefully perched on it, almost as if expecting it to collapse like in the old Goldilocks tale. He gave her an approving nod, but didn't coax out a smile.

"Okay now." Brett clapped, getting the attention of the still-jabbering children. "When I say the words *little red schoolhouse...one, two, three,* what do we do?"

"We see who can go the longest without saying anything," Betsy piped up, proud that she knew the answer.

Abby's eyes widened as she stared at him in disbelief. Catching on now, was she?

"Does the winner get a prize?" one of the visitors demanded, his freckled face screwed up in concentration at the challenge ahead.

Brett's Jeremy had sported freckles, too. Blond hair and the biggest blue eyes, just like his mama. "There's no prize. But it's fun, so we don't need prizes."

The boy didn't look convinced, but Brett pulled up another tiny chair and sat down, too. Then he leaned forward to clasp his hands on the table and the children likewise clasped theirs. After a slight hesitation, Abby followed suit.

"Are we ready?"

Nods all around the table. A giggle from Mary garnered her a glare from the others.

"Okay, here we go. Say it with me." He made eye contact with each eager face, making sure all were on board. This was such a fun age. Or it could be when kids were healthy and whole, not laboring for every breath drawn into fragile lungs.

"Little red schoolhouse..." a chorus of childish voices chimed in with his. "One...two...three."

Blessed silence descended as each child pressed lips

tightly together, watchfully peering around the circle of faces in search of the first culprit to break the quiet.

As the blissful moments stretched, a broad smile appeared on Mary's face and several others pointed accusingly, hands clamped to their own now-smiling mouths to keep from saying anything.

"She's still in the game," Brett assured softly. "She hasn't said anything."

Mary gave them a "so there" look, lips tightening with renewed resolve. Brett winked at Abby, who slowly shook her head. He imagined she'd remember this crowd control ploy for some time to come. It was so quiet he could hear a baby crying in the nursery across the hall.

Abruptly, the boy who'd demanded a prize gave a loud, overly dramatic gasp and gulped in mouthfuls of air. "I can't breathe!"

Initially startled, the other kids stared with rounded eyes. Then almost in unison, they cried out in grinning triumph. "He talked!"

"You don't hold your breath, silly," red-haired Skyler admonished with a sigh of disgust. "Can we start over, Brett? He's doing it wrong."

Brett leaned over to pat the visitor on the back, making sure he was okay. He was fine, but liked putting on a show.

"That's right, don't hold your breath. You can breathe through your mouth or through your nose or…through your ears if you want to."

The kids giggled.

Mary plugged her ears with her fingers and made a face of distress. "I can't breathe! I can't breathe!"

The room erupted in laughter, and Brett caught Abby's eye. She was laughing, too, and his heart unexpectedly lurched. Man, was that glimpse behind the starchy-mannered exterior worth waiting for.

The now-composed boy grinned. "I won't hold my breath again. I promise."

"We'll play one more time." Brett again caught their teacher's eye. "Then I believe Miss Abby here has a Bible story for us and probably something fun to make to take home."

Abby nodded and the kids turned to look at her as if noticing her for the first time. Another round of the game and the kids were settled down enough to focus on a Bible lesson. All except Skyler, that is, who gave Mary's pony-tail a tug. Brett hauled him into his lap and, after a half-hearted struggle, the boy finally relaxed against him, a too-familiar weight and little boy scent that brought back memories. Wrapping his arms around Skyler's waist, Brett rested his chin atop the soft thatch of hair and nodded for Abby to begin.

David and Goliath. A bittersweet heaviness settled into Brett's chest. Wouldn't you know it? One of Jeremy's favorite stories. Right up there with Noah and the ark, Jonah and the whale, and Daniel in the lion's den. Thankfully the Lord had gotten hold of that precious boy's daddy just in time or he'd never have heard those stories—or about how Jesus loved the little children.

Brett swallowed, forcing away the past as he concentrated on the woman in front of him. She recited the story slowly, with enthusiastic animation, as she moved magnetic cutout characters across the whiteboard. The gentle voice, tinged with a slight huskiness that lent it a distinction of its own, held the children riveted.

Brett shifted Skyler on his lap, as captivated as any of the kids. His ex-wife, Melynda, never read Bible stories to Jeremy. She'd wanted no part of God after the cystic fibrosis diagnosis, and no part of her husband, either, once Jeremy passed away. Brett didn't often allow himself to dwell on those dark times and God had been faithful to ease the relentless, piercing pain of loss. So why today?

If there was anything he'd learned over the past seven years since losing Jeremy and the shock of his wife's departure, it was that there were good days and there were bad days. On both, he could only thank God for allowing him to have a wife and a son in his life for as long as He had—and take another step into tomorrow without them.

Abby had never seen anything quite like it. The man had merely entered the classroom and suddenly the world was all about him. Or the children's world anyway. Even when at the hour's conclusion they'd gathered up their papers to await their parents, Brett had once again become the focus of their attention and she was all but invisible.

Had she known Brett went to Canyon Springs Christian, she wouldn't have been so easily persuaded to take on Meg's Sunday school class. It wasn't that she didn't appreciate how he'd settled the children down with that clever schoolhouse game of his. She'd been on the verge of panic before his arrival. But really…had he needed to remain through the entire lesson? Help out with the crafts? Not that she wasn't grateful for the assistance, but his watchful eyes, teasing remarks and knowing smiles had made it harder on her, always wondering what he was going to do next.

That was one thing she'd appreciated about Gene, her steady-as-he-goes fiancé. Twelve years her senior, the long-widowed university professor was a man of fixed routine and predictability. A creature of habit. No surprises there. Or at least that's what she'd thought until he broke off their engagement, annoyed that she'd be unable to fulfill her part of the marital bargain and had messed up his carefully laid plans to father a child of his own. He'd acted as if it hadn't been as equally a painful blow to her.

Brett saw the last of the kindergartners off with a wave, then turned to where Davy had joined her to help gather materials back into his mother's canvas bag. Snatching up a roll of paper towels, the cowboy moistened a few in the room's corner sink, then wiped down the tables with every bit as much enthusiasm as he seemed to lavish on anything he set his mind to. Which, she had to admit, could be irritating. Must be nice not to have a care in the world.

But why did he keep hanging around? Didn't he have any place he needed to be?

Slinging the lesson bag over her shoulder, she patted Davy on the back. "Why don't you find Grandpa? I'm sure he'll be expecting you in church."

Davy's brow wrinkled. "You're not coming?"

"No, I have a few things to attend to. But I'm sure your grandpa will see that you get lunch and bring you home afterward." Or at least that's what he used to do when she was a kid.

Even though only the Diaz children—not the adults—had actually attended church, Dad enjoyed Sunday family times and they'd given his wife a break from meal preparation. Mom still hated cooking. Dad had done much of it whenever he could, so they'd probably consumed way too many meals prepared on his oversize grill and Sunday specials at Kit's Lodge.

"You'll still be there when I get home, won't you?" Davy's eyes sought hers for reassurance. Thank goodness his mother would return this afternoon. Abby was already losing her heart to this little guy and he seemed to be latching on to her, too.

"I'll be there. Me and that shoe-chewing pooch of yours."

Davy grinned, then with a wave to Brett he disappeared out the door.

"Good kid." Brett retrieved his hat from atop the supply cabinet, a version that was in more pristine condition than the one he'd worn at the equine center yesterday. He'd donned his Sunday best, too—well-oiled boots, dark jeans and a crisp white Western-cut shirt. "So how's his mom and the *bambina?*"

So that's why he'd lingered. He wanted an update on Meg.

"She and the baby are both stabilized and she's hoping to come home this afternoon. She can't return to work, of course, but at least she may be able to wait things out at home."

"Glad to hear it." Rotating his hat in his hands, he didn't seem in any hurry to be on his way.

She patted the bun on her head, ensuring it was still secure, then took a step toward the door. "Thank you for helping out. That little red schoolhouse thing is ingenious."

"I was more than happy to assist." He cocked his head, eyes twinkling. "But I thought you librarians knew all the tricks in the book about kid control. Assuming, of course, they still have story hours at libraries these days."

Abby shrugged. "I was a high school librarian."

"Was?"

Ugh. He'd picked up on that slip of the tongue.

"Yes, was." But she didn't intend to discuss it. Cutbacks in funding weren't kind to a private school librarian with a paltry four years of experience. Even with a master's degree, she'd been among the first to be let go at the end of the spring semester.

In the weeks since school ended, she had no idea how she'd managed to motivate herself to apply for the few available librarian job openings in the Tucson area, let alone make a good showing in the interviews. Nevertheless, she hoped to hear an affirmative for the fall semester soon. It didn't much matter which one. With an apartment to maintain and car and education loans to pay off, she couldn't afford to be choosy.

Eyeing her curiously, Brett nevertheless didn't press her for an explanation, for which she was grateful.

"There you are." A masculine voice came almost accusingly from the doorway. Her dad. The stocky, mustached Bill Diaz stepped into the room, wire-rimmed glasses perched on his hawklike nose and salt-and-pepper hair highlighted by the fluorescent overhead lights.

"Hey, Bill." Brett stepped forward to shake his hand.

He knew her dad?

The older man's smile broadened. "I should have known you'd manage to find the prettiest girl in the building."

Brett darted a look in her direction, the first uncomfortable one she'd seen coming from him. Had he naively assumed she hadn't already heard of his ladies' man reputation and thought Dad was spilling the beans? He must have forgotten she'd observed him with the women at the equine center and borne the impact of his heart-stopping grin.

Brett sheepishly returned her father's knowing smile. "Somebody's gotta keep an eye on them. Keep the rounders at bay."

"You're the man for the job, son." Her father gave him a nod of approval, then turned to pin Abby with a frown. "What's this Davy's saying about you not staying for church? Come on now, folks are wanting to see you again. Since you're staying the weekend after all, you need to give your old man a chance to show off his beautiful daughter."

Why was Dad being so jolly this morning? When they'd last spoken as she packed her car on Saturday morning—before Meg's SOS to help with Davy's riding lesson—things had been extremely awkward. "Dad, I don't want to be shown off."

"Indulge me. Sit beside me during the worship service and join me and Davy for lunch at Kit's."

Her hopes lifted. Did he want to put more effort into bridging the gap of too many lost years? To try again to establish a relationship with his long-absent offspring?

Then she remembered Sharon.

"I don't want to intrude."

He lowered his glasses on his nose to peer at her. "Intrude? On what?"

She cast an uneasy look in Brett's direction. He didn't need to be privy to family matters. "I assume Sharon's joining you?"

Her father's brows took a dive. "She's not. She has a ladies luncheon to attend. But what if she *were* coming? She wants to get to know you better, honey, just like I do."

"Dad—"

"You can bring your friend here, too." He waved his hand toward Brett.

Brett wasn't her friend. He wasn't her anything. "Dad, I don't—"

"You both have to eat, don't you? My treat."

Brett shook his head. "Thank you, sir, but—"

"Come on, join us. Abby needs to get to know some young folks in Canyon Springs. Maybe you can talk her into staying a few weeks. Maybe all summer."

Hope flickered. Dad wanted her to stay? It sure hadn't felt like that yesterday morning. He'd seemed as bewildered as she was about how to build a real-life bridge between them, not just communicate through birthday cards and an occasional ill-at-ease phone call. The past few days she'd spent with him had seemed, well, more than weird. And disappointing. Maybe he'd been disappointed, too?

"Come on, Brett," Dad urged again, almost as though needing an ally in the struggle to find comfortable ground with his only daughter. A third party to balance things out?

While her instincts warned to stay away from Brett—
he was a heartache waiting to happen—his presence at
lunch might ease the tension between her and Dad. He and
Davy would keep conversation at a superficial level and
his happy-go-lucky approach might deflect the wounding
sparks that sometimes flared between father and daughter. Despite her misgivings, Brett's accompanying them
suddenly seemed vital to paving the path to a harmonious
connection with Dad.

Brett's eyes narrowed as if trying to read her thoughts,
then he dropped his gaze to the hat in his hands. "I appreciate the invitation, Bill, but I'm sure Abby can make up
her own mind as to how long she wants to stay in town."

He moved toward the door.

"You're welcome to come." Her rapid response provoked a surprised lifting of a brow as his gaze met her
now-pleading one. Couldn't he see that just as he'd barged
into the Sunday school class, he needed to barge in here
now, too? Needed to be a buffer between her and Dad?

Come on, cowboy. Say yes.

Chapter Four

Monday morning Brett rolled over with a groan and felt around blindly on the nightstand for his ringing cell phone. Six o'clock. It was his day off, but he'd overslept by two hours. He had someplace he had to be. Early. Before the wind picked up.

"Brett?"

He recognized the voice of his sister Geri, one of the twins. Two years older than him, both sisters sported red hair, a sprinkling of freckles and energy that wouldn't quit. He collapsed back on his pillow. "What's up?"

"It sure doesn't sound like *you* are yet. Oversleep?"

"I forgot to set the alarm." A Singing Rock emergency had ensured he'd gotten to bed late, then he'd lain awake too long kicking himself for not taking Bill Diaz up on his lunch invitation yesterday. Abby had clearly wanted him to come with them, as he'd interpreted it anyway, to be a buffer between her and her father. Not a spot he cared to be in. But it had eaten at him the rest of the day, second-guessing his decision not to go along. He'd wondered about Abby's sadness when he'd first met her and it seemed likely the father-daughter relationship played a role in it. There had been an evident tension between the two of them in the brief interchange he'd witnessed.

"You have to plan a weekend at Mom and Dad's sometime soon," Geri insisted. Despite being the bossier of the twins who often acted like a second mom to him, she was the sibling he felt closest to. Even though she had a look-alike playmate, she'd nevertheless loved joining him in his childhood adventures and they developed a special bond. Through the years Geri had become—and remained—his confidante.

"That's not on my agenda. Why?"

"Amber, Erin and I were thinking about getting everybody together. We haven't all been in one place since Thanksgiving. Maybe you could stop in Ashfork and pick up Grandma and Grandpa on your way."

He scrubbed his free hand over his face, cognizant of the morning stubble along his jaw. A Marden family get-together at the ranch his folks managed was always an event to look forward to. He hated to miss out.

"You know summers are the busiest time of the year for me. That popular blog that's been featuring our town jump-started the tourist season early, too. We have a lot of events scheduled at the equine center, and here at Singing Rock we're already filling up." He worked part-time at both locations, having been fortunate enough to snag accommodations as a part of the deal at the cabin resort, where he was usually on call evenings. "I'm still picking up work on the side and the kids' camp is coming along, too."

For a long moment his sister remained silent.

"What?" he prompted. But he could guess what she was thinking. He'd heard it enough times from all three sisters. And Mom. His three older brothers and Dad weren't so disapproving of his choices.

"You're still burying yourself in your work, Brett."

Readying for a lecture, he reluctantly pulled himself up and propped the pillow against the headboard, behind his back. "It's called being fond of eating and having a roof over my head. Oh, and providing the same for that spoiled horse of mine."

After a too-long time in the city, it had been a joy to have a horse of his own again and to hit the forested trails surrounding Canyon Springs. Just him, Cinnabar, Elmo and God.

"I'm not making light of your situation, but it's been seven years since you lost Jeremy and Melynda left you. Care to share when you're going to let yourself have a life again?"

He had a life. Maybe it wasn't how the happily married Geri with her two rambunctious kids thought it should be. But he had a good life. Interesting work and a kid-oriented project occupied his time, involvement with children being a step he'd once thought he'd never again choose to take.

"Does anyone there even know what you've been through? Offer support?"

He'd shared bits and pieces of his past with Janet Logan, who'd skillfully and compassionately pried them out of him. A no-nonsense, practical type, she hadn't fawned over him and his losses. No stranger to heartache herself, she could be counted on to keep private what he'd confided to her.

"I've mentioned it to a discreet, older lady from church. But you know I don't like people knowing my business."

Geri made a scoffing sound. "Doesn't that strike you as odd? I mean, you are one of the most open, gregarious men I know. Yet you're still keeping all of this to yourself."

"I don't imagine hearing about it would brighten anyone's day." It hadn't brightened Janet's by any means, but her grandson's challenges with cystic fibrosis had built a strong bond between them.

"Maybe not, but you're not allowing anyone outside the family to serve as a support system. Don't you dare tell me doing that is 'a guy thing.'"

Why couldn't the females in his family leave him in peace? He shook his head and leaned over to turn on the nightstand lamp even though sufficient sunlight peeped in around the edge of the curtains to make it an unnecessary effort. "I don't need a support system. I'm doing fine. God is good. Life is good. And I'm better than good."

Considering what he'd been through, that was the truth. He was happy…for the most part. Enjoying life. No, maybe it wasn't all he'd once dreamed of, but did anyone ever have it *all?* Doubtful.

"You still aren't seeing anyone, are you?" Not surprisingly, her tone rang with accusation. "No one special, I mean."

Special. That meant letting a woman get close enough that you cared when she walked out. "In God's time, Geri. I'm in no hurry to run ahead of Him."

He hadn't even been much tempted to. No woman had caught more than his slightest interest in a long time. Unbidden, the image of Abby Diaz reading the Sunday school lesson to the kindergarteners slid into his sleep-fogged mind. He could picture how the kids sat rapt, listening to the animation in her somewhat husky voice—a voice that could get under a man's skin real quick if he let it.

He ran a hand through his hair, dismissing the memory.

"Maybe you've barred the door to God's plan," his sister persisted. "Have you ever considered that?"

He swung his legs over the edge of the bed and stood, the hardwood floor cool under his bare feet. He needed to replace the rug his overgrown pup, Elmo, had chewed up last week. "So now you're evaluating my spiritual life?"

"Of course not. But a man who is looking for a wife—"

Where'd she get that idea?

"—doesn't move to a town with a population of less than three thousand souls and hide out with his horse."

He cracked a smile. "I lived in Phoenix for five years

before coming here. Fifth largest city in the country, with probably half the population female."

"And the whole time you were there you were hanging on to the hope Melynda would come back, so you didn't date even then."

"I was doing what I believed God wanted me to do." Working full-time to pay off the medical bills and taking classes on the side didn't cater to an active love life.

"If you hadn't been funneling money to Melynda through her folks," she chided, "maybe you could have paid the bills off sooner. Her folks blindsiding you with the news that she'd gotten pregnant and remarried proves she didn't deserve your help."

Brett held back the growl forming in his throat. Geri *would* have to remind him of Melynda carrying another man's child. But helping his ex-wife financially was something else he'd felt led to do even though it hadn't been a requirement of the divorce settlement. Up until two years ago when she'd remarried, he'd never thought of her as an ex. After all, he'd signed on for the long haul even if she hadn't. He'd hung on to the belief that if she saw him living a convincing life of faith, walking in Jesus's footsteps, she'd eventually give her life to God, too, and find her way back to her husband.

That had been his prayer anyway.

Hearing a robin's insistent chirp, he moved to a window of the one-room cabin and pulled back the curtain to a day well on its way. His day off and he was already burning daylight.

"Face it, Geri. I could move to a planet populated entirely by women and not meet Ms. Right if it's not in God's timing."

"You have to at least give Him something to work with. Canyon Springs is beyond remote."

He let the curtain drop and headed to the kitchenette to

get coffee started. "You've forgotten that Mom and Dad's pastor met his better half on the mission field in Peru. God picked up another missionary and plopped her right down in the middle of that remote mountain village. When the time is right, it happens."

She gave an exasperated sigh. "I'm not saying God can't do anything He wants to. I'm just saying—"

"That you love me and you want me to be happy." He picked up a ceramic coffee mug from the stack of dishes in the sink, rinsed it and set it on the counter.

Her voice softened. "You're such a wonderful guy, Brett."

"I know. I try not to let it go to my head."

She snorted. "I'm serious. You deserve to have a woman who loves you. You're so good with kids, too."

"I'm an uncle times fifteen, does that count?" With six siblings, the youngsters had added up fast, now aged four through nineteen years.

"It counts, but…you were such a great dad."

Silence hung momentarily between them as they reflected on unspoken memories of son and nephew.

"Thanks, Geri." He'd like to think his child had a father he could count on, that Jeremy had known he was loved beyond measure. Yeah, he'd see his boy again when he himself departed this world, but he'd long harbored a dream that he might one day hold another of his children in his arms in the here and now. His sisters meant well but, unfortunately, tended to forget one critical factor.

He again picked up the coffee mug, scrutinized it, then rinsed it out a second time. "It's awkward to bring up in casual conversation with a woman you've just met that you're a carrier of the defective cystic fibrosis gene. Even harder to suggest it might be a good idea that she get tested before a relationship progresses too far."

He'd tried that once with a classmate he'd become friends with after Melynda remarried—it hadn't gone over well. But the truth of the matter was that if both partners were one of an estimated ten million who were carriers of the flawed gene—as had been he and Melynda—each time you got pregnant you had a 25 percent chance of having a child with CF.

He couldn't lose another child like that again.

"I'm aware it's a challenging situation," Geri resumed with a gentler tone. "But I'm praying and so is the whole family, that you'll find your Ms. Right. Soon. Sometimes when I pray, I feel such an expectation that it won't be long."

A smile twitched. "Even if I'm hiding in Canyon Springs?"

"It's a long shot," she teased back. "But like you said, God can do whatever He wants. Just promise me, Brett, that when your Ms. Right shows up you won't sneak out the back door and hit the road running."

Most of the women he'd met here in town were married, engaged or obviously not a good match for any number of reasons. Like Britney Bennett. Or they were tourists briefly visiting mountain country to escape the heat in other regions of the state or visiting family. Like Abby Diaz.

He'd heard at Camilla's Café last night that Meg hadn't come home from the hospital yesterday after all. Which meant Abby might still be in town today...

He leaned back against the counter, the scent of coffee in the making luring him closer to a waking state. His big sis wanted him to promise not to sneak out the back door and hit the road running, huh? "We'll see."

"Brett! You have to cooperate. You know God doesn't strong-arm us into His will."

Would not canceling his commitment to paint Joe Diaz's garage today be considered cooperating? He didn't have any designs on his friend's sister, but Abby would only be here for another day or two at most. He still felt bad about ducking out on lunch yesterday. It wouldn't hurt to check in on her.

"We'll see," he said again, tamping down an unexpected flicker of anticipation. "We'll see."

"Davy! Breakfast is ready!"

Abby poured a glass of milk for her nephew and set it on the kitchen table. Then she popped a striped straw into Davy's glass and stepped back to view her handiwork. What would he think of the colorful table setting she'd thrown together? She'd woven a place mat from wide strips of yellow and lime-green construction paper and cut out the toast with a round cookie cutter to make a smiley face. A blueberry-eyed peeled banana now stood on toothpick legs.

Davy had been disappointed when Joe came home late yesterday afternoon only long enough to shower and head back for a shift of work. His mother hadn't come home at all—the doctors wanted to keep her another night for observation. But maybe the whimsical breakfast table would start his day on a positive note and after school his mom would be home.

She could hear him bumping around upstairs, but she hadn't let the dog in last night so that shouldn't be the cause of his delay this morning. Is this how Meg always started her day? Trying to get out the door to work while rounding up a foot-dragging Davy? Nevertheless, Abby couldn't help a twinge of envy. Meg was mother to an adorable stepson and soon to give birth to a baby girl. Would Jori have Joe's smile? Meg's eyes?

"Here I come!" Davy hollered, footsteps pounding as he clambered down the stairs. He dashed into the kitchen, then came to a halt in front of the table, eyes wide. "Is it your birthday or something, Aunt Abby?"

She laughed. "No. I thought you might enjoy an extra happy breakfast."

"My toast has a jelly smile," he pointed out as he pulled out a chair and sat down. "Can I eat it?"

"Yes, you can eat it. I'll dish up your oatmeal when you're done with that."

"Awesome. Is Brett coming to breakfast, too?"

She certainly wouldn't invite Brett to breakfast, especially not after he'd turned down the invitation to lunch yesterday. She couldn't decide if she was more disgruntled with him for not helping her out when she'd practically pleaded or with herself for looking to a stranger to ease tensions between her and Dad.

"What makes you think he'd be coming to breakfast?"

Davy leaned over to grasp the strings attached to the drapery rod and drew back the curtains of the French doors overlooking the patio. He pointed to the detached two-car garage at the rear of the spacious treed lot. "I saw him from my window upstairs."

Sure enough, there was Brett, a cowboy hat topping his head as he hauled a ladder from the back of a gray pickup. What was he doing here? Shouldn't he be on his way to work?

"Maybe he's hungry." Davy took a bite of his toast. "Brett's always hungry at the church potlucks."

Abby looked down at the festive table, where she'd been about to join Davy. Toast. A banana. Soon-to-be oatmeal. Hardly enough to sustain a man the size of Brett.

She moved closer to the glassed door. "Where's he going with that ladder?"

"Dunno."

She watched a moment longer, then returned to the stove to stir the oatmeal. "Go ahead and eat. He won't be expecting breakfast, and you need to finish getting ready for school."

Davy took another bite of toast, then again leaned back in his chair for a better view of what was going on outside. "Oh, man, he brought Elmo."

"Who's Elmo?" She doubted a *Sesame Street* character had accompanied Brett but, if the sudden onslaught of barking was any indication, she could almost guess the answer.

"His black Lab. He and Camy are best friends." Davy stood up. "Look at her. She's going crazy to get out of her pen."

Abby moved to the door once more, then looked up at the wall clock. Seven-fifteen. The neighbors probably *loved* the canine serenade, but the two young dogs did seem particularly pleased to see each other, tongues lolling as they cavorted on either side of Camy's enclosure.

"Sit down and eat, Davy. You can't be late for school."

"I don't want to go to school." But he nevertheless slumped back into his chair. "Nobody would miss me if I stayed home and played with Camy, Elmo and Brett today."

She again returned to the stove and dished up a bowl of oatmeal, then set it in front of him. "There are three more days of school left and these last days before summer vacation are always the most fun. I doubt Brett and Elmo will be here long. It looks like he's dropping off a ladder for your dad."

Davy didn't look convinced.

They were finishing breakfast—Davy had only to eat his banana and he'd be done—when a knock came at the back door off the utility room.

"Brett!" Davy jumped up, but she reached out to stay him.

"Sit down, please. I'll get it. You just eat." Meg and Joe were trusting her with Davy. She couldn't allow him to be tardy on the one day she saw him off to school. Not surprisingly, when she opened the door Brett stood on the back porch, hat in hand.

To her irritation, her heart beat faster at the sight of his cheerful smile.

"Mornin', ma'am. Sorry for the ruckus a bit ago. I guess the pups were happy to see each other."

"I got that impression, too, as I'm sure the neighbors did, as well."

His eyes sparked with amusement. "I thought I'd better stop by and give you warning that Elmo and I'll be around the property painting Joe's garage today."

Didn't he have a job at the equine center? "So your dog's good with a paintbrush?"

A dimple surfaced. "Probably as good as I am, sad to say."

She glanced over his shoulder toward the building in question. Joe hadn't mentioned Brett would be doing handyman work. From where she stood, the garage didn't look like it needed paint. But what did she know? "So, you're telling me this will be a 'pardon me, ma'am' day?"

He cocked his head in question.

"That's what my mother calls it when you have a re-pairman popping in and out interrupting you. You know, pardon me ma'am but may I borrow a wrench? May I use your restroom? May I have a drink of water?"

Brett grinned. "I shouldn't need any wrenches."

But he'd be underfoot all day. She glanced again at the garage. Did it truly need sprucing up? "It's nice of you to paint Joe's garage."

His eyes twinkled. "Not really. He's paying me."

Should she invite him in? Offer a cup of coffee to start his day? She couldn't afford to have him engage Davy in lengthy conversation and risk making him late for school.

"Do you want my banana, Brett?" Davy called from the kitchen table, just out of the cowboy's line of vision.

Brett's amused gaze momentarily caught hers, then he called back. "Thanks. But I've had breakfast. That banana's all yours."

"I don't like bananas."

Great. He'd kept quiet about that.

"This one has legs, too."

Brett raised a brow and she nodded.

"And eyes," Davy added.

As Brett's disbelieving gaze questioned her, Abby sighed and stepped back from the open door. "Come on in. You may as well see for yourself."

Chapter Five

Brett toed off his boots outside the door. He'd been briefly to Duffy's that morning only long enough to feed Cinnabar and didn't want to track anything untoward into the house. But from the look on Abby's face, it was clear he'd only been invited to step inside because of Davy's bidding and he'd better not plan to linger long.

Following her trim, jeans-clad figure into the kitchen, he got the impression she preferred the events of her day to be well-ordered, like library books categorized by the Dewey decimal system. She was probably one of those who had her own personal reading materials grouped by author or subject and probably had them inventoried on a spreadsheet that noted publishers and copyright dates. While he was an avid reader, his books were stacked in no particular order wherever he found empty space. Dresser top. Back of the closet. Corner of the living room floor.

"See?" Davy pointed to an arch-backed banana with toothpick legs and raisin feet, then he poked the milk glass straw in his mouth and took a long swallow. "Aunt Abby made him."

Brett placed his hat atop the refrigerator, then pulled out a chair from the table. He whipped it around backward, straddling it and crossing his arms along the back.

A smile twitched as he took in the colorful breakfast trappings. "That's some critter you have there. I'm impressed."

"You can have it." Davy scooted the plate toward him, then glanced at Abby. "I already ate the smiley-face toast and oatmeal. Do I have to eat the banana, too, Aunt Abby?"

She glanced up at the clock, a crease forming across her brow. "No, that's okay. I didn't know you didn't care for bananas. You need to let me know what you like and don't like so I don't fix things you won't eat."

If he'd had any doubts before, that nailed it. Leaving a door open like that labeled her an amateur when it came to kid dealings. He could almost see Davy's mind whirling. Likes: ice cream, hot dogs, pizza, French fries. Dislikes: spinach, green beans, peas—and bananas.

The boy pushed the banana plate closer to Brett. "My mom is going to have a baby."

"So I heard."

"I think everybody's having babies, like at church and the grocery store and stuff. You can tell because the moms get big, big, big." That matter-of-fact wisdom shared, Davy drank down the remainder of his milk before setting the glass onto the table with a clunk. "I'll be right back, Brett. I have to brush my teeth. It's a school day."

The boy scrambled to his feet, then dashed out of the kitchen and up the stairs.

With a grin, Brett reached for the leggy banana. "Observant kid. I have to admit it does seem like every other woman in town is in a family way. A Canyon Springs population explosion."

Unfortunately, for the past few days every time he saw one of those moms-to-be, he couldn't help but be reminded of the nine months he and Melynda had eagerly awaited the arrival of their precious Jeremy.

Abby glanced at him uncertainly. "You don't have to eat the banana if you don't want to."

He studied it for a moment, the beady, unblinking eyes almost appearing to look back at him. "I think I'll give it a try. I've never eaten anything quite like this. Special occasion?"

She shrugged, looking a tad sheepish. "I was trying to start Davy's day on a bright note. He misses his mom, and Joe didn't get to stay long yesterday."

"I'd heard Meg's return was delayed, that she'd probably be released this afternoon."

Surprise lit Abby's eyes. No doubt she didn't yet recognize the effectiveness of the Canyon Springs grapevine.

"That's what we're hoping," she said almost cautiously. "Her doctors want to keep an eye on her awhile longer."

"Whatever it takes to ensure a safe delivery." He pulled the toothpick legs from the banana and placed them on the edge of the plate, then motioned toward a chair at the table. "Have a seat, Aunt Abby."

She hesitated, almost like a filly shying away from something unfamiliar. He didn't usually spook ladies, but this one seemed more than skittish this morning.

"I'm not a coffee drinker." She motioned to the unplugged coffeemaker on the counter. "So I haven't started any this morning. But would you care for a glass of orange or apple juice?"

There, that was better. A glimpse of her more hospitable side.

"Thank you, ma'am, I would. Apple juice, please." He broke a bite-size chunk from the banana.

She headed to the refrigerator. "Could we drop the ma'ams, please? I'm beginning to think you have me mixed up with your great-grandmother."

"Believe me, there's no chance of that." He cast her an admiring glance and noted with satisfaction that color stained her cheeks as she returned to the table to pour his juice. "But attempting to take the ma'ams out of me is a losing battle. My mama and daddy ingrained that into me."

"Calling me ma'am makes me feel ancient."

"Can't have that." He tipped an imaginary hat. "So I'll do my best—ma'am."

She shook her head, the faintest of smiles touching her lips. Headway. She sat down across from him, placing clasped hands in her lap as if drawing on the depths of her patience to wait for him to consume his snack and get on out of there.

"So," he said, studying her as he broke off another piece of Davy's cast-off fruit, "did you enjoy lunch with your dad yesterday?"

Her brows almost imperceptibly lowered, apparently not caring for his choice of topics. But he was still curious about the sadness he'd read in her eyes, guessing it had something to do with a misunderstanding with her parent.

"It was okay."

"You don't get to see each other much, I take it."

"As in never. Or hardly ever, anyway." She reached for her own glass of juice.

"Bill hopes you'll stay in town longer." He'd quickly picked up on that.

She lifted the glass to her lips and took a sip. "I intended to, but it's not a good time for Dad to have company with the summer crowds descending. He's super busy getting them settled in, I need to get back to Tucson anyway."

Had he correctly picked up that Sharon Dixon's presence played a part in the change in plans, as well? A match between Bill and Sharon seemed inevitable, but a sure thing might have gotten muddy if Abby had voiced objections.

"How long have you lived in Tucson?"

She glanced out the French doors and for a moment he

thought she wouldn't respond—or at least that she'd tell him to mind his own business.

"Since I was ten."

Which explained why Joe may not have mentioned a sister who was never around. "This other brother. Ed? He lives down there, too?"

"Sometimes." She rose from the table and carried her glass to the sink.

Okay. She didn't want to talk about it. Brett finished off the banana and juice just as a dressed-for-school Davy trotted into the room, a backpack slung over one shoulder.

"Will you be here when I get home, Brett?"

"Maybe. Why?"

"I thought you, me, Camy and Elmo could play Frisbee together."

"If I'm still here, we'll do that. But I may have other things to take care of this afternoon."

Davy's mouth drew downward, then he turned to Abby with hopeful eyes. "Will you be here?"

Brett got the impression the boy hadn't been told details of his mother's anticipated return, not wanting to get his hopes dashed if that didn't work out.

"Yes, I'll be here."

"Good." Davy trotted over and impulsively gave her a hug, then he turned back to Brett. "Aunt Abby is the best."

She ushered Davy into the living room and out the front door. By the time she returned, Brett had cleared the table, rinsed his glass and was drying his hands on a towel looped through the refrigerator door handle.

"I'd best be finding myself a paintbrush." He reached for the hat he'd earlier placed atop the fridge, not missing the relieved look in Abby's eyes at his announcement. She followed him to the back door, where he stepped outside to pull on his boots.

"I thought you'd be working at the equine center today," she said almost accusingly, "not painting garages."

"Day off."

"Oh. Then I hope your painting goes well."

And that he'd finish as quickly as possible and hit the road?

"Thanks. And thank you, too, for broadening my life's horizons."

She tilted her head.

"You know," he prodded, hoping to provoke a smile, "the banana. That's the first one with eyes and legs I've had the pleasure of consuming. It was made more tasty, too, by the lovely company it was shared with."

She met his gaze with an unsmiling one of her own, unmoved by his compliment. He must be losing his touch. But while he hadn't quite gotten to the heart of her underlying melancholy, he'd glimpsed some light-in-the-window evidence in a colorful place mat, smiley-face toast and a banana with legs.

No, she wasn't encouraging him to stop in again throughout the day. But he'd see about that. She still looked as if she could use a friend.

Abby peeped between the curtain panels of the window over the kitchen sink. Where had "the cowboy," as she'd come to think of Brett, gotten off to? Although she hadn't heard his truck start up, signaling his departure for lunch, the cheerful whistling had stopped, not to resume this time. The big pickup still hunkered near the garage, but Brett was nowhere to be seen. No sign of Elmo or Camy, either.

As long as he stayed out of her hair, that's all that mattered though, right? Stepping away from the window, she surveyed the kitchen she'd cleaned that morning. She'd scrubbed floors, wiped baseboards and oiled cabinets. In fact, she'd tackled anything in the house she could think of that might make life easier in the coming days for her sister-in-law—and keep her mind off thoughts she was better off not dwelling on.

She avoided the baby's room.

Saturday night Davy had proudly insisted she join him in admiring his new sister's space. Yellow-and-white-checked curtains complimented a baby bed and changing table in a rich, polished oak that matched the rocking chair. A woven rug coordinated with a cheerful turquoise blanket, and diminutive dresses and one-piece outfits hung on kid-size plastic hangers in the closet.

Despite the big brother's enthusiasm, Abby hadn't lingered long.

This morning she'd kept both mind and hands occupied as all the while the windows had remained open to the cool, fresh mountain air. Each time the whistling stopped out back, she'd held her breath, expecting to momentarily hear a knock at the door and find Brett on her doorstep. On one hand, keeping to himself was thoughtful. But on the other hand she found it irritating, leaving her to wonder when he'd inevitably put in an appearance. And why he'd stopped whistling.

She appreciated the fact that he hadn't engaged Davy in lengthy conversation that morning, diverting him from getting ready for school. But she hadn't wanted to talk about the glut of pregnant women on the streets of Canyon Springs or life in Tucson far from her father and brother. Nor did she care to discuss the uncomfortable relationship she currently shared with Dad. Was it less than a week ago that she'd crammed the trunk of her car with enough clothes for a month or more, naively intending to step back into her childhood role as "daddy's little helper" at the RV park and campground?

Dad didn't need a little helper now. He had Sharon.

Her cell phone chimed and, after another quick peek

out the window and a relieved confirmation of the caller ID, she picked it up from the countertop.

"Hi, Mom."

"Abigail, John and I are off to New York to celebrate my birthday." Abby's heart warmed at her mother's excitement and she pictured her still youthful-looking parent's slim figure, upswept dark hair and expressive gray eyes. "There's a musical on Broadway I've heard nothing but good things about and John says our favorite hotel has snagged one of the city's most innovative chefs."

"That sounds fun." John was the man Mom married eight years ago, a successful businessman who delighted in indulging the whims of his wife. "You'll be gone a few days?"

"A week. Maybe two."

That figured. Mom had volunteered to look after Abby's apartment while she was gone, keeping the plants watered and the fish fed. Maybe she could track down her brother to check on her place—he'd understand their mother's capricious last-minute decisions if anyone did. So would Mom's long-time cook and housekeeper.

"Be sure to leave my key with Alicia, then, will you?"

Her mother moaned. "I promised to take care of your place, didn't I? I'm sorry, honey. John has to go to New York on an extended business trip and we decided I should go along."

"That's okay. I won't be staying in the northland much longer anyway."

"Do I hear regret?" Her mother gave a sympathetic sigh, rightly interpreting her daughter's words. "I warned you not to get your hopes up about the town and your father. Things are seldom as you dream they'll be."

Wasn't that the truth?

Abby wandered from the kitchen into the living room of the Craftsman-style house, noting with satisfaction how the wooden surfaces she'd polished glinted in the light and the air smelled of tangy lemon oil. Between working full-time and the effort of carrying the baby, Meg clearly hadn't kept up with the household chores. Joe had probably done his best, but he worked full-time, too, and any time at home was better spent with Meg and Davy.

"How *is* your father doing, Abigail?"

Abby stared out a window to the quiet, tree-lined street. "He's seeing someone."

"I'm not surprised and you shouldn't be, either. It's been eighteen years since we went our separate ways."

But why'd he have to find someone right now?

"A local woman, I assume," Mom continued, "and not someone he found on an internet dating site?"

The latter was hardly her dad's style and Mom knew it. But it was one more example of how different the two of them were. Abby's mother had met John online. "He's seeing Sharon Dixon, who owns Dix's Woodland Warehouse. You remember her, don't you?"

"Sharon," her mother repeated thoughtfully. How did it feel to know she'd been replaced? "At least she grew up in Canyon Springs like your father did. She fits in, which is more than I can say for myself. While I managed for over fifteen years, I couldn't take it any longer. So I'm delighted for him, and you should be, too."

"She's definitely nothing like you."

"Then good for Bill." Mom sounded genuinely pleased. "He and I mixed like the proverbial oil and water. He'd never be happy with a clone of me, so don't take it too hard, sweetie. He was bound to find someone else eventually."

"I know. The timing just stinks. I hadn't planned on sharing Dad this summer." She'd had such foolishly high hopes.

"What about Joe? Have you seen him? I assume the baby hasn't arrived."

"No, not yet. But soon." There was no point in going into the complications of the past few days since it appeared that all would end well. "Joe works long hours, so I haven't seen him much, either."

"I know you wanted more from this trip," her mother sympathized as Abby heard John call to her in the background. "I'm sorry, sweetheart, I have to run. I'll give your key to Alicia right now."

"Thanks, Mom. Tell her it won't be for long."

"You said you may be coming home sooner than planned. You may want to reconsider that. Your former fiancé keeps calling to ask how he can get in touch with you."

A knot formed in Abby's stomach. Months ago she'd tearfully confessed to her mom the truth of his departure.

"I wouldn't put it past him to make a nuisance of himself when you come back." Mom sounded protective. "Not an ounce of patience, that man. He would have made a terrible father. You're well rid of him."

While she intellectually knew that to be true, for months after the breakup she'd hoped and prayed he'd rethink things, her spirits skyrocketing every time the phone rang, only to plummet when it wasn't him. But last week, when caller ID first confirmed him as the caller, she couldn't bring herself to answer the phone. If he said he'd changed his mind about them, would she be open to that or was it a door better left closed?

"If he wants to get back together, don't let him wear you down, Abigail. Even if your father would have followed me to the ends of the earth, I wouldn't have changed my mind about returning to him and Canyon Springs."

On that cheerful note, she and Mom said their goodbyes and Abby returned to the kitchen, where not long ago she'd sat uneasily at the table with Brett. Now she again found herself listening for his cheery whistle and, almost with a sense of relief, she heard it once again.

What did he have to be so happy about anyway? It must be nice to have a carefree life. She again peeked between the curtain panels over the sink. Elmo and Camy had flopped down in the nearby shade, but Brett was halfway up the ladder doing something near the roofline, the sun beating down on him. As she watched, he pulled out a handkerchief, then lifted his hat to wipe his brow before settling it once more on his head.

An inner prompting niggled at her. It had warmed up considerably since he'd arrived that morning. He must be getting hot. Thirsty. Yet he'd taken the hint and not bothered her. Not even once.

Please don't ask me to go out there, Lord.

Brett would probably, egotistically, take it personally, assuming, as he'd audaciously surmised on Saturday, that she'd found something that caught her interest.

She let the curtain fall closed and stepped back from the window.

No way was she going out there. She wouldn't give him the satisfaction.

Chapter Six

"I totally understand, George." His cell phone wedged against his ear, Brett frowned critically at the plastic he'd taped over a garage window. "But we're in a bit of a bind."

"You know I'd like to help you and Mrs. Logan," the physician who'd returned his call continued. "It's a great project. But my kids are wild to spend a week at Disney World and your dates fall right on top of it."

"I sure don't expect you to cancel your plans." It was nearing noon and he'd yet to crack open a can of primer. He'd been on and off the phone most of the morning since Janet Logan called him with disheartening news. "Do you know other doctors who might fill in for us? Or maybe two or three who could split the week's commitment?"

He'd urged Janet months ago to get a backup, maybe two, but she hadn't heeded his suggestion. The doctor she'd scheduled had been part of the camp for years, but she hadn't counted on him being laid up from a car accident.

"I'll check here at the hospital," George continued. "And make a few phone calls."

"If you can get the word out that we're in need of a doctor on the premises, it would be appreciated."

When they'd finished their conversation, Brett shut off the phone and clipped it to his belt, then he gazed up at the brilliant Arizona-blue sky and spread his arms wide. "Now what, Lord?"

"Let me know if you get an answer."

Startled at the feminine response, Brett turned to see Abby headed his way with a big glass of clear, icy liquid in her hand. Well, what do you know? He hadn't had to storm the gates after all.

Elmo and Camy galloped off to her, tails wagging, while Brett adjusted the hat on his head and enjoyed the view as Abby gracefully approached. She halted before him and held out the glass with mock solemnity.

"Pardon me, ma'am," she said, lowering her voice to a manlike tone, "but may I have a drink of water?"

He grinned and reached for her offering. It looked like biding his time had paid off. Grandma always said good things come to those who wait. "You must be a mind reader, Abby. It's warming up out here."

"You should have said something earlier."

He'd keep it to himself that if he'd gotten desperately thirsty, he could have used the outside spigot to fill the thermos jug he kept in his truck.

She glanced down at the two Labs still dancing eagerly around her, then knelt to pet them. "I'll get Elmo a bowl, too. I imagine Camy has an extra one around here someplace."

"I'm sure he'd be much obliged." Brett tipped the glass to his lips, the cool, refreshing liquid coursing down his throat.

Elmo gave Abby's jaw a lick and she laughed, a rare lighting of her too-often serious expression. Then she glanced up at him apologetically. "I couldn't help but overhear the end of your conversation. You need a doctor for something?"

"For a weeklong camp for elementary schoolkids who have mild-to-moderate physical disabilities. It accommodates twenty-five kids from around the region each summer."

"Wow. That sounds worthwhile."

"Totally. Janet Logan—you met her on Saturday—started it five years ago."

"Actually, I met Mrs. Logan before Saturday. She was the school librarian when I lived here and my Sunday school teacher, too, can you believe it?" She gave the dogs a final pat and stood. "What prompted her to start something like the camp?"

"Her grandson, who'd been born with disease-related challenges, reached an age when he couldn't easily join in with other kids on camping expeditions that are so popular around here. So she decided to do something about it."

"That take-charge spirit sounds like what I remember of her. In fact, I believe she mentioned on Saturday something about wanting to recruit me to work at a camp this summer."

Now that would be sweet—but way too distracting.

"The program must have taken off fast," Abby added, "if it involves that many children."

"I'm sure the parents of even more kids would take advantage of it if additional resources were available." That was his and Janet's dream anyway. Jeremy would have loved the camp. One of his first words, spoken while pointing longingly out the screen door of their ranch house, was *outsidey.*

"An organization sponsors it?"

"Janet's mostly done it on her own, making the arrangements, recruiting volunteers, drumming up monetary support and making sure everything meets state and local requirements."

"So how did you get involved?"

Brett tensed at the unanticipated question. Jeremy. But he wasn't telling her about that.

Abby held up her hand before he could pull his thoughts together for a suitable response. "No, let me guess. You sign on for anything to do with kids."

"You got it." *Nice catch, Lord.* "Last year was a heart-breaker for Janet when the camp had to be canceled. The property owner sold it and she wasn't given enough notice to find a new location. Places book up years in advance around here and few are suitable for kids with physical disabilities."

"So lots of disappointed kids."

"Right. Janet contracted with a new place for this year, but the doctor who partnered with her in the past had an accident over the weekend."

"And you can't find another one."

"I'm hitting dead ends so far, but I'm determined to see that Janet and the kids get their camp this year. The new property is quite a few miles outside town, off a rugged forest service road. It's fairly remote because she wants the kids to have an authentic camping experience, not the equivalent of pitching tents in a city park."

"Which means you want a physician in-house."

"Exactly." He squinted one eye and looked to her in ex-aggerated appeal. "You don't happen to know one with a big heart, do you?"

Something indecipherable flickered through her eyes. "No. I'm afraid not."

"Keep your ears open for a willing doctor or two. We'd be obliged."

"I…can do that." But she didn't sound hopeful and abruptly turned away to study the structure behind him. "It didn't look like it from a distance, but I guess the ga-rage does need painting, doesn't it?"

She'd doubted the legitimacy of his reason for hanging out here today? Mistrustful little soul.

"It's seen better days. I've sanded rough places and

hammered in wayward nails. Washed it down. Next comes primer if the wind holds off." He took another drink and deliberately caught her eye. "If you're finished with that vacuuming I heard, you can give me a hand out here."

Her eyes rounded. "Me? I'm no painter."

"You have an artistic bent. I saw that from your breakfast table this morning." *Thoughtfulness, too, and sensitivity to a boy's feelings.*

"Believe me, you'll accomplish your chore much more quickly without me."

She had a point there. He wouldn't make much progress with his gaze drifting to hers and to that hourglass figure she sported. Attempting to coax out one of those rare smiles demanded his full attention, too.

"The invitation stands. But you must already be keeping yourself occupied. I'm the same way. Unless I'm given an assignment, I'm at loose ends when I'm visiting other folks for a few days."

"Meg didn't give me an assignment, but I wanted to leave her a freshly cleaned home before I head back to Tucson."

"She'll appreciate your efforts. Joe, too." He nodded toward the house, the prospect of Abby's imminent departure not brightening his day. "You'll leave as soon as Meg gets back?"

"I might stay tonight to make sure she's settled in."

She eyed the half-full glass in his hand as if willing him to hand it over so she could be on her way. He clenched it more tightly and took another swallow.

"I want to thank you again," she suddenly hurried on, "for helping out with the Sunday school class yesterday. A lot of guys—and gals—would have taken one look at the chaos and run the other direction. You're good with kids."

"They tolerate me."

A disbelieving laugh lit up her features. "That's putting

it mildly. They were all over you the moment you stepped in the door. Kid magnet."

"Hey, you held them rapt with your talent for storytelling, too." Brett grinned at the memory. She'd sure enough held *his* attention. Then and now.

Just promise me, Brett, that when your Ms. Right shows up you won't sneak out the back door and hit the road running.

His smile faded at the remembrance of his sister's words. Abby wasn't his dream woman. He wasn't even convinced there would ever be one or that he'd have the heart to saddle a woman with his personal baggage. Besides, Abby wouldn't be here but another day at most so there would be no God-led future in that direction. *Sorry, sis.*

Nevertheless, he slanted a look at her. "Do you have plans for lunch?"

From the startled expression in her eyes, she hadn't expected that from him. He wasn't sure why the words popped out of his mouth. Maybe the recognition that she'd be leaving tomorrow promised no pressure or expectations on either of their parts. What could be safer than that?

Was Brett asking her out?

"I—"

The intrusive rumble of a blue extended cab pickup truck drew their attention as it rolled to a stop behind Brett's vehicle.

What was Dad doing here?

He climbed out and waved, then headed in their direction. "Joe phoned to tell me he remembered Brett might be coming to work on the garage today. He asked me to drop off my scaffolding to help with that peak above the garage doors."

"Thanks." Brett shook hands with her father. "But it's

not surprising Joe would forget considering what's going on with Meg."

"That's a fact." Dad turned to Abby with an expectant look. "Your brother says the doctors want to keep her at the hospital at least until the weekend."

The weekend? No, no, no. Her spirits momentarily faltered at the prospect of remaining longer in Canyon Springs, then her heart jumped in alarm. "Why? Has something happened? Is she okay?"

"She's worn-out. Lab work came back somewhat off and her blood pressure's still on the high side. They want to keep her and the baby monitored. It's not like Canyon Springs is a block away from the hospital. Joe thinks they're concerned about the distance and don't want her to get into another emergency air-vacc situation."

Abby grimaced. "I hope her insurance company cooperates with that precaution."

"Me, too, but I expect a few extra nights is less expensive than a 'copter ride." Dad perched his glasses farther down on his nose to study her. "Joe planned to phone you himself, but got called out on a paramedic run right as he was finishing up with me. He wanted to ask if you'd stay with Davy until Meg returns. I told him that wouldn't be a problem, that you—"

"Dad!" Now he was making decisions for her as he'd done when she was a kid. "I can't stay in town indefinitely."

He shrugged. "Why not? It's summertime. You're between jobs. What's your hurry?"

She lowered her voice, thankful that Brett had discreetly moved closer to the garage to inspect his handiwork. But he was still within earshot.

"I talked to Mom this morning. Something's come up and she can't watch my apartment for me." Dad raised a brow slightly, no doubt thinking the same thing she had.

Mom not following through on a commitment wasn't anything new. "Besides, I need to continue the job search in case the positions I interviewed for fall through. I should meet with my academic advisor, too, about registering for the second summer session."

Dad's brows lowered. "So you're determined to remain in the Tucson area."

Surely he didn't think she intended to move back to Canyon Springs. And work *where?* Camilla's Café? Kit's Lodge?

"It's been home for a long time."

"Too long in my opinion." Dad folded his arms. "I still don't see what it would hurt to stay and help your brother out. It's a great opportunity to spend time together."

She bit back an exasperated laugh. "I've been here for days and I've barely seen either of you. His job's demanding and his family needs his attention. Besides, why can't Meg's brother and his wife step in? You forget, I'm a total stranger to Davy. While I'm flattered Joe and Meg trust me with him, I imagine he'd love to stay out at Singing Rock if it's anything like I remember. His uncle Rob could take him fishing at the creek or something."

Dad gave an adamant shake of his head. "That's too disruptive. With his mother hospitalized, the boy needs to be in his own home and in his own bed at night. It's going to be enough of an adjustment as it is when that new baby sister puts in an appearance."

"But, Dad—"

"Sometimes family needs to come first, Abby."

She drew in a sharp breath. "Then why don't you come stay with him? Surely seeing to the welfare of your grandson isn't that big of an inconvenience."

The words were out of her mouth before she could stop herself, their implication charging the atmosphere between them. At the look on her dad's face, Abby immediately regretted her sharp tongue. When Mom had taken off with Abby and Ed, Dad seldom drove to the southern part of the state to visit, even in the winter off-season. When he did, it was for a brief, often disappointing time spent at some neutral spot like a fast-food restaurant or park. But that reminder should have been better left in the past.

Her father removed his glasses and leveled on her the same stare she remembered from childhood when she'd disappointed him. He didn't have to say a word. Guilt had always eaten at her when he gave her "that look." It still had that effect on her.

She sighed. "I don't see—"

"I'm not trying to make the decision for you—"

Oh, yeah, right.

"—but think it over and let Joe know. He'll be swinging by later to pick up a few things for Meg. But if you can't do it, I'm sure Sharon would be happy to help out."

Her eyes narrowed. Sharon. Now that wasn't fighting fair and he knew it. Yes, she was a dear friend of Meg's but this was a family matter. Obviously, no answer but "yes" would win her a place in her father's good graces.

"Brett." Dad glanced toward the cowboy, who was still inspecting the garage. Or at least pretending to. "Let's get that scaffolding out of the truck."

"Yes, sir." Brett stepped forward and held out the now-empty glass to her. "Thank you again, Abby. That hit the spot."

"You're welcome. I'll put a bowl for Elmo on the back steps."

He nodded, then turned to follow her father, but she hadn't missed the fact that the customary twinkle in his eyes had been absent.

She stared after the pair as they moved to the back of the pickup truck. Well, that was nice. Now Brett knew she was jobless, that she didn't think family was important and that her father disapproved of her. *Thanks again, Dad.*

Brett would be especially impressed if he knew she was a phone call away from an ex-fiancé whose physician sister had a history of volunteering her services for church-related kids' events—but Abby had no intention of contacting Gene about that.

Elmo bumped against her leg and she knelt to give him a pat. What did it matter what Brett thought of her anyway? He wasn't anybody special in her life. It didn't matter one way or another if he thought she was a good daughter and a reliable sister. He could judge her all he wanted, but the truth was that she barely knew Dad and her brother now, let alone her sister-in-law.

So give me a break, cowboy.

She gave Elmo a final pat and stood, watching the overgrown pup gallop off after his master. Then she headed toward the house, her thoughts drifting to the minutes before her father had driven up. Things had started out awkwardly when she'd first brought Brett a glass of water. She hadn't known what to say to him. But gradually, she'd relaxed—until he asked her if she had plans for lunch. Was that a prelude to asking her out?

And more importantly, what would have been her response?

Chapter Seven

Too much wind had prevented Brett from priming the garage the previous afternoon. With dust kicking up and dry, brown pine needles raining down, he'd have ended up with a mottled mess had he attempted it.

But remembering Davy's wistful request to play Frisbee, Brett swung by the house not too long after Davy got home from school the following day. He'd found the boy in the front yard romping with Camy, and was unaccountably relieved to see Abby's car still parked by the side of the house. He'd tried not to listen in on the conversation between her and her dad yesterday, but it was hard not to catch snatches of it. Divorce sure did a lasting number on relationships that went far beyond the husband and wife association.

Joining Davy in the yard, he unsnapped his shirt cuffs and rolled up his sleeves. Then he clapped as Camy raced Elmo for the Frisbee Davy had flung, leaping into the air to catch it in her teeth. As she brought it back to Davy, Elmo trotted along beside her, trying to pull it away. Brett grabbed the black Lab and wrestled him playfully to the ground.

"You're gonna have to work harder, fella. She's fast on her feet."

Davy held out the slobbered-on blue disk. "Your turn, Brett."

"When do we get a turn?" Ace Logan called as he and his two companions trotted across the driveway from an adjoining yard. The boy and girl nodded excitedly in agreement.

"Well, get yourselves on over here." It never ceased to amaze him how kids appeared out of the woodwork wherever he went, hungry for a man's time and attention. Dads—and often moms—didn't seem to have time for their own kids anymore like his parents had for him.

He motioned the girl forward. She couldn't be much over seven. Maybe eight. A smile lit her face as she ran straight to him in confident trust. He glanced toward the neighboring house, hoping an adult was keeping a watchful eye on her from behind the curtained windows and knew he was one of the good guys.

He squatted next to the brown-eyed charmer. "What's your name?"

"Hannah."

"Well, Hannah, I'm Brett."

Davy pointed at the two boys. "You already know Ace, and this is Anthony."

"Welcome, Ace. Good to meet you, Anthony." He shook their hands, noting with concern that Ace seemed winded, then he turned his attention to the dogs capering around them. "Looks like these two are ready to play."

As he showed Hannah how to throw the Frisbee, his heart swelled at the precious gift of children. There had been a time when he'd withdrawn from them, even pulled away from his nieces and nephews, but thank God that time had passed.

Elmo and Camy galloped around the yard as one by one he helped the kids keep a Frisbee airborne long enough for the dogs to capture the flying disk. Eventually a familiar voice called from down the street and Ace paused. "That's my grandma. I have to go."

He took off. Hannah and Anthony lingered longer, then they too reluctantly headed home. It was then that Brett spied Abby sitting on the steps of the front porch.

Her dark hair, tied back with a ribbon, fell over one shoulder and sandaled feet peeped from under an ankle-length skirt. He'd left his hat on the steps and now it nestled on her lap. Whoever coined the phrase "pretty as a picture" must have had Abby Diaz in mind.

"How long has your aunt been there?" he whispered to Davy as he handed him the disk for another throw. Davy had been generous sharing the Frisbee with his friends, so he deserved a few more throws before they, too, called it a day.

Davy shrugged. "Dunno."

Brett raised his hand in greeting. She waved back. Then he slipped his arm around Davy's shoulders and showed him how to get more power into his throw. The dogs galloped off after the Frisbee. After a few more rounds, Davy fist-punched the air.

"They both caught it at the same time! Did you see that, Aunt Abby?"

"I did!"

Camy and Elmo trotted in circles, both still gripping the plastic disk and playfully trying to attain sole possession of their prize. Davy hurried off to claim it, but Brett made his way across the yard to where Abby sat.

"Those two pups," she pointed out as she handed him his hat, "are going to sleep well tonight."

Brett grinned as he settled the hat on his head. "Likely Davy, too, if I didn't get him too wired up."

"He was disappointed when he got home and discovered his dad had been here and gone, so this has been good for him."

"Joe's back at the hospital?"

"He wanted to see Meg himself, not rely on a 'don't worry, I'll be fine, honey' phone message. I hope, though, that he can get some sleep tonight. His hours are so erratic that I don't know how he can keep going like he is."

Brett propped a booted foot on the bottom step. "You're still here, so I take it you'll be spending more time in Canyon Springs?"

"Looks like I'm stuck."

Stuck. Not a happy word. Nevertheless, he gave her an encouraging smile. "Your loss, my and Davy's gain. What changed your mind?"

She brushed a ladybug from the hem of her skirt. "Dad knew once he said Sharon would step in that I'd cave."

"I'm surprised you don't care for Sharon."

"It has nothing to do with her personally, it's just that…" She allowed her gaze to travel across the yard to where Davy wrestled with the pooches. "I came up here last week, thinking I'd stay awhile to help Dad at the campground, get to know him and Joe better. But when I got here, there was Sharon looking right at home at his place."

"You didn't know he was seeing anyone?"

"No. I made a mistake by not calling ahead and telling him I was coming." Seeing the question in his eyes, she continued, "I was afraid if I called ahead that he might tell me not to come. Or if I changed my mind before I crossed the city limits that I'd let him down by backing out at the last minute. So I just showed up and it caught him off guard, just like Sharon's being there caught me off guard."

"The two of them have been seeing each other quite a while. It's gotten to be that you don't expect to see one without the other now."

"So I hear." She rested her elbows on her knees and propped her chin on the heels of her hands. "You must think I'm behaving like a two-year-old."

"Why would I think that?"

"I mean, I'm a grown woman and my folks have been divorced for longer than they were married, yet I'm not dealing well with a new woman in my dad's life."

"Once you get to know her, you'll get used to the idea and give your wholehearted approval."

"I hope so. She was nice to me when I was a kid and stopped by Dix's to pick up a loaf of bread or a gallon of milk for Mom. But I also remember her as a gruff-sounding chain-smoker who dumped her daughter off at church on Sundays so she could have some peace and quiet, like my folks did with Joe, Ed and me."

"A lot can happen over time. You've been gone a number of years."

"I know. But it seems weird coming back here and finding things so different than they used to be. Out of kilter." She crossed her arms and rubbed her hands up and down them, as if warding off a chill. "I mean, it's like being in the middle of a book and anticipating the outcome, only to discover halfway through that a chunk of pages is missing and new ones from some other story are wedged in where they don't belong."

"You've been bucked off and landed hard."

"That's an interesting way of putting it." Relief at being understood sparked in her eyes. "When I ran into Sharon's daughter a few nights ago, she seemed to take it for granted we'll soon be stepsisters. But *my* version of 'the book' didn't include the chapters where all that came about."

"I know it's disorienting at the moment, but you'll fill in those missing chapters."

Abby shook her head with a self-deprecating laugh. "I probably sound crazy to you, don't I?"

"Not at all."

"I usually keep my own counsel."

He could relate to that, and he had no trouble accepting that Abby was telling the truth when she said she kept herself to herself. Even though on the surface she seemed to be a capable enough young woman, from their first meeting he'd sensed a fragileness about her, a vulnerability. Something that called to him to step in and protect her from whatever might threaten. Like a roomful of overactive kindergartners? But it was extreme to think she needed protecting from Sharon Dixon.

Abby glanced at her watch and stood. "I guess I'd better call Davy in for supper. I'm not used to having a kid around who's on a school-night schedule. Quite honestly, I'm amazed his parents are trusting him to me. I mean, while Joe and I have been in contact more often in recent years, he and I haven't been close since I was a kid. Meg doesn't know me at all."

"I think their trust is well-placed. You're conscientious and responsible, and Davy seems to have taken to you. You called me a kid magnet, but you're a kid whisperer yourself when it comes to your nephew."

She didn't looked convinced.

"Aunt Abby! Save me!" A laughing, panting Davy rushed up to them, the pups on his heels. He scrambled onto the porch and held the Frisbee aloft, out of the reach of the leaping dogs.

Brett snagged the disk from his hand, then flung it across the yard. Camy and Elmo bounded after it.

"Man, thanks, Brett. They kept jumping on me so I couldn't get away to throw it."

"Looks like they could both learn some manners," Abby pointed out. "But there's no time to address that tonight. Supper's ready."

"All right!" Davy raised his hands in celebration. "I'm starving. Come on, Brett. It's time to eat."

Abby's gaze met Brett's uncertain one. How was she supposed to get out of Davy's invitation? She couldn't. At least not without appearing rude.

"There's plenty for all of us." She offered a hesitant smile to Brett as Davy dashed past her and into the house.

"You're sure?"

No, she wasn't sure at all. But she had too much Diaz in her not to be hospitable. "I am if you like spaghetti with meat sauce, salad and homemade bread."

"*Homemade* bread? That's mighty tempting, but I don't want to intrude on your time with Davy."

"He misses his dad, so I think he'd like having you here for guy talk."

As the dogs raced back and flopped, panting, at the bottom of the steps, Brett whipped off his hat and motioned toward the front door. "If that's the case, you've twisted my arm. Lead the way, ma'am."

She cut him a warning look.

"Abby." He cracked a smile as he toed off his boots and left them at the door.

The aroma of tomato-rich spaghetti sauce and freshly baked bread scented the air as they stepped inside. Brett gave a low whistle. "Now that's a smell a man dreams of coming home to."

Keep on dreaming, cowboy.

"You can sit next to me, Brett," Davy called from the kitchen, where he'd already seated himself at the empty table. He pointed to one of the other chairs. "Aunt Abby sits there like Mom does, so she can dish up the food easier."

"Actually…" From where she and Brett stood just inside the front door, Abby glanced uneasily at Brett. Maybe her plan to end Davy's day on a cheery note wasn't such a good idea now given their unexpected company. It seemed kind of silly. "I thought it might be fun to eat in the living room. You raced right by it, Davy."

The boy hurried back to the doorway separating the kitchen from the front room, confusion in his eyes.

Abby pointed toward the seating area where she'd arranged the wicker trunk coffee table with two blue-checked place mats awaiting Meg's snow-white stoneware. Best of all, three of Meg's chunky battery-operated candles—part of a wedding gift set from Abby—formed a centerpiece atop an oval mirror. Davy had earlier confided that his mom gave him authority over lighting her candles, so she'd placed the remote control by his red cloth napkin.

He trotted over to the makeshift dining table, snatched up the remote control and lit one of the candles. Turned it off, then on again. "Awesome, Aunt Abby."

Brett placed his hat on the back of the sofa, then rested his hand lightly on the boy's shoulder. "Looks like a table set for a king, Davy."

"I'm king of the remote." Davy waved the electronic device in triumph, then, as if reminded of his manners, he held it out to Brett. "But I'll let you light one if you want to."

"No thanks, buddy. You're the man in charge tonight." Brett shot Abby an amused glance.

She cringed inwardly. He probably thought she was a nutcase. Bananas with legs and now shunning chairs and incorporating remote controls for mealtime entertainment. "We can move all of this over to the table. We don't have to eat sitting on the floor."

"An adventure in dining is fine with me." He winked at her, but his assurance didn't set her heart at rest. Quite the opposite.

"Please sit down, then," Abby encouraged, eager to step into the kitchen and still the butterflies now swooping through her stomach. Having company tonight—Brett—hadn't been a part of the plan. She'd have done things differently, would have dressed nicer. "I'll get supper served up."

"I can help with that."

To her dismay, Brett followed her into the kitchen.

"Like I said—" she motioned helplessly "—we don't have to sit on the floor. That's something I thought would be different enough to keep Davy's mind off his folks being gone."

"I wouldn't miss out on this for anything." Brett pulled out stoneware plates and wooden salad bowls from the cabinet she directed him to. "Pasta. Homemade bread. And that remote control is a stroke of genius. You sure know the way to a man's heart."

His gaze locked momentarily with hers. Flustered, she turned to the stove. He was talking about Davy, right?

Brett moved around beside her, his arm brushing hers as she lifted the lid on the pasta. "I still can't get over the fact that Joe has a sister. He and Meg have wedding photos all over the place, but he's never pointed you out."

"That's because I'm not in any of them." She shrugged as though it were of no consequence, then dipped the pronged spoon into the spaghetti noodles. "I couldn't make it to the wedding. Prior commitments, unfortunately."

Very unfortunately. She'd spent an awkward week in rain-soaked Seattle with Gene and his parents only to have him dump her by year's end.

Brett reached for the filled plate and set it aside, then handed her another. "I managed to make it to all my brothers' and sisters' weddings. No trivial feat considering I have six of them."

She gasped. "You're kidding. Seven kids? That's a houseful."

"We had enough room, thanks to bunk beds. My family has managed a ranch in west-central Arizona for several generations. Cattle. Horses. Growing up we had our fair share of chores, but it was a kid's paradise."

"I'm jealous." She filled the plate, then handed it back to him and filled another.

"You grew up at Bill's campground, didn't you? I can see how there would be fun in that, too."

"It was. In some ways, anyway." As a kid, she'd thought of the campground as her own Disneyland. "I liked interacting with the summer visitors—quite a few kids my age—and helping Dad. I followed him around like Elmo probably does you."

Brett was a sharp guy. It had to be obvious to him that something had changed between father and daughter somewhere along the line.

"I was an Elmo with my dad, too." He placed the last filled plate aside, resettled the lid on the pasta pot and lifted the lid on the meat sauce. "We spent a lot of time together. While he occasionally shot baskets and played catch with me like other fathers did, mostly we worked side by side. Baling and hauling hay. Moving cattle from one part of the ranch to another. Feeding in the winter. Vaccinating. Mending fences. I wouldn't trade those years for anything."

"Do you still get along? You're still close?" She ladled sauce over the steaming noodles on each plate, hoping she didn't sound as wistful as she felt. With a big happy family like the one he grew up in, no wonder Brett could whistle while he worked and smile at the world.

"The whole extended family is close-knit. Grandparents. Uncles. Aunts. Cousins. Nieces and nephews."

"Lucky you." Would she have bonded more deeply with her own extended family if Mom hadn't dragged her and Ed off to Tucson? Dad could at least have had them spend a few weeks up here with him each summer. Maybe cousins like Olivia or Reyna—the pastor's wife—would have become her best friends?

Stifling a sigh, Abby set aside the ladle and headed to the refrigerator for the Parmesan cheese and an oversize bowl of salad she'd prepared that afternoon. Leaf lettuce. Fresh spinach. Celery and red peppers. Sliced olives. Thank goodness she'd made more than enough, thinking she'd have it for lunch the next few days and use the left-over spaghetti sauce for lasagna, another of Davy's favorites.

She glanced back at her guest, ridiculously charmed at the way he was studying, kidlike, the engraved design on a salt shaker he'd picked up from the countertop. But the ripple of muscles along his forearm as he placed it back where he'd gotten it was a sharp reminder that he was all man.

Above all else, guard your heart, she reminded herself, *for it is the wellspring of life.* That Bible verse probably came with a footnote referencing Brett Marden.

"Davy tells me you're always hungry," she said, filling in the conversational gap.

Brett drew back in exaggerated surprise. "How'd he figure that?"

"Church potlucks."

"A spy in our midst?"

"Apparently so." She set the salad bowl and cheese on the counter, then again reached into the fridge for the glass of milk she'd already poured for Davy and an ice-cold carafe of water. "There's plenty of food tonight, so don't feel as if you have to take mouse-size portions."

"That's good to know, because as mouthwatering as this smells, I doubt I could be counted on to mind my manners."

He disappeared into the living room with the spaghetti-filled plates and she could hear the engaging rumble of his voice and Davy's higher pitched one. *Please let this evening be over quickly and painlessly, Lord.* It served as a thank-you for Brett's helping out at Sunday school and spending time with Davy this evening. Nothing more.

She'd finished slicing the still-warm bread when Brett returned.

"I hope you have extra batteries, Abby. Davy's got the shades pulled down and those candles going like one of those dancing light shows."

With a laugh, she reached for a nearby drawer handle and pulled it wide, revealing several packages of assorted batteries. "I anticipated that."

Brett shook his head, his eyes aglow with admiration. "Mom types must have a sixth sense for this kind of thing."

She pushed the drawer closed, avoiding Brett's gaze.

Mom type.

That wasn't the first time this evening he'd alluded to her alleged parenting instincts. A year ago she'd have laughed at the idea that modern men gave much thought to potential childbearing and nurturing skills when shopping for a mate. But she'd had an eye-opener in recent months, learning the hard way that she was now permanently barred from meeting critical aspects of that much-desired criterion.

She briskly handed Brett the salad bowl and Parmesan, then picking up the cloth-lined basket of warm bread, Davy's milk glass and the carafe, she injected her next words with a cheeriness she didn't feel. "Looks like we're ready to eat."

Avoiding his gaze, she slipped past Brett and into the living room with its now dimly lit—and undeniably romantic—candlelit ambiance. Or it would have been if the flameless candles hadn't been flashing like strobe lights.

Eat fast, cowboy.

Chapter Eight

"Father God, we thank You for the many blessings You give us daily. The things we notice and the things we pay little mind to. Thank You that Davy's mom will be home soon and that his aunt Abby is here in the meantime. Thank You for the food she's fixed for us."

Amens echoed around the wicker trunk table, then Brett reached for the bread basket from the makeshift buffet he'd arranged on two adjoining dining chairs. He held it out to Davy. "Still warm."

Davy set aside the remote control to help himself, then Brett held the basket out to Abby, noting that the faux candlelight further softened her delicate features and glistened on her dark hair. She seemed on edge tonight and, although she'd welcomed him to join her and Davy for a meal, maybe he shouldn't have accepted the invitation. After all, it had been Davy's impromptu idea, not Abby's.

"Do I get to gallop this week, Brett?"

He set aside the bread and passed the salad to Abby. "There won't be any galloping until the end of summer, Davy."

The boy propped his elbow on the table and settled his chin into his palm. Then he stabbed at his spaghetti with a fork. "How come?"

"Davy." Abby shook her head and Davy lowered his elbow from the table.

The boy's brow wrinkled. "Why don't I get to gallop?"

"We have to make sure both you and your horse are kept safe." Brett started in on his salad. "There's a lot to learn when you're dealing with an animal that big. With twice a week classes this summer, you'll get plenty of opportunities to ride. But a full-out gallop will come last."

"Bummer." Davy's lower lip drooped, then he abruptly sat up straight. "Aunt Abby knows how to gallop horses, don't you, Aunt Abby?"

Brett glanced at her. This little librarian with not so much as a hair out of place was a horsewoman? "I want to hear about this."

A soft smile touched her lips. "You may not be pleased with what I have to say."

"Impossible."

Abby took a bite of her salad and chewed thoughtfully, as if deliberately drawing out the suspense. "I ride English style. Not Western."

Brett placed his hand over his heart and drew back to eye her in mock disapproval. "Blasphemy."

She laughed. "Didn't I say you wouldn't be pleased?"

"What's blaffomy?" Davy demanded, not quite able to get the word out correctly.

"It means," she said, amusement lighting her eyes, "that Brett doesn't think that's real riding."

"How come?"

Brett leaned forward, fixing his attention on Davy. "You can't stay seated in a saddle the size of a postage stamp when cutting out a calf from the herd. Or roping one. Where are you going to tie that lariat without a saddle horn?"

"Ah, but I can jump a fence in that stamp-size saddle without the risk of burying a saddle horn in my stomach."

She added dressing to her salad, seeming to enjoy razzing him. "And I don't break my back lifting when I'm saddling my horse."

"You have a point there." Brett cocked his head in acknowledgment as he launched into his spaghetti. "So when did you learn to ride? Do you ride often?"

If she already had a comfort level with horses, she might be trainable. Balance and confidence working with horses were transferable skills, but she'd have to be broken of that ridiculous posting to a trot habit and adapt to one-handed neck reining.

"I started when I was in middle school," she continued. "I begged Mom for riding lessons and actually did some regional showing when I was in high school and college. But I haven't ridden since I graduated."

"We'll have to see what we can do about that, then." He turned to Davy. "I talked to your dad today and he's okayed a hat and boots. So how about a shopping trip? We can get you outfitted before next week's lesson. Both of you."

Davy cheered, but Abby shook her head. "Oh, no, I'm not the cowgirl type."

"Come on, you'd put any rodeo queen to shame."

Davy nodded. "Yeah, Aunt Abby. You can get one of those hats with sequins."

She laughed. "Oh, no, not me."

"What do you say to tomorrow afternoon? It's Davy's last day of school, isn't it? Those are usually half days. I'm working tomorrow evening at Duffy's, so I'll have the afternoon off."

"Please, Aunt Abby?"

Yes, please, Aunt Abby. For whatever reason, the thought of spending the afternoon with her appealed.

"I suppose if your dad's on board…"

"All right!"

"Looks like we have a date, then." Brett's smile broadened until he caught the startled look in Abby's eyes. "A shopping date, I mean. I'll pick you both up here after school lets out. We can head to Show Low for a late lunch. How's pizza sound? Then we'll hit the ranch and Western-wear stores."

"Only if I don't have to buy a sequined hat."

He studied her a long moment, savoring the teasing sparkle in her beautiful eyes, then nodded. "Deal."

Laughing, she reached for her fork just as her cell phone chimed, but she made no move to answer it.

"Better check it out. It might be Joe or Meg."

Almost reluctantly she pulled the phone from her pocket and glanced at the caller ID. Grimaced.

"Telemarketer?"

"No. But no one I want to talk to." She returned the phone to her pocket, the set of her mouth still grim.

He hoped it wasn't her dad. But the openness he'd glimpsed during the few minutes since they'd settled down to eat had once again shuttered. For the remainder of the meal, he and her nephew carried the conversation. She listened as Brett told tales of growing up on his folks' ranch and Davy chatted on about horses, school and how his dad was the strongest man in the world. But Abby contributed little and Brett couldn't reengage her or entice a smile.

They'd barely finished carrying the remains of their feast to the kitchen and putting leftovers away when the doorbell rang.

"I'll get it." With Abby occupied loading the dish-washer, Brett headed for the front room, still puzzled as to how to draw her out. Who'd that phone call come from?

He opened the door to find Janet Logan on the porch, a foil-covered, lasagna-size dish in her hands.

"I thought that looked like your truck, Brett." She didn't sound the least bit surprised to see it here, but held out the dish to him. "This isn't hot. It goes in the freezer. Enchiladas, one of Joe and Davy's favorites. When Meg gets home she won't want to do a bunch of cooking."

He reached for the dish. "As one who's been privileged to enjoy your fine cooking, I'm sure this will be appreciated."

"This goes with it." She produced a can of enchilada sauce from the woven bag draped over her shoulder and placed the can on top of the dish. "Any word on a substitute doctor yet?"

"Not yet. Everyone says it's too short of notice."

"That's not breaking news for either of us, is it? I should have listened to you about arranging a backup."

The hopelessness in her voice wasn't characteristic of Janet and he rallied to encourage her. "I'm not giving up yet and you shouldn't, either."

"Less than three weeks until the camp starts isn't much time and we can't wait to call it off the day before everyone arrives."

"No, but we'll figure something out. Don't you worry."

The post–Memorial Day flood of summer visitors into town had him putting in some odd hours, and it was only so late at night you wanted to call a physician asking for a favor. He should have taken care of camp business tonight instead of playing Frisbee with Davy and accepting an invitation to dine with a pretty woman.

"How's Ace doing, Janet? He seemed fine on Saturday, but when he was over here before supper, his breathing didn't sound good. Like mucus was hanging up in his lungs."

"You don't miss much, do you?" She angled a sharp look at him. "He doesn't want to miss the last few days of school to go to the specialist in Phoenix. So his dad's working with him each night to get things loosened up inside."

Not a pleasant ordeal for father or son.

"Tell Alan and Hollie not to wait too long. These seemingly innocent episodes can take a sudden turn." No chance that they'd get caught out in the middle of nowhere in a two-day snowstorm like he had with Jeremy, but you could never be too careful.

"They'll go down on Friday, so stop your worrying." Janet's unusually stern voice gave away her concern for Ace as well as the reminder of Jeremy. Not long ago she'd mentioned putting in for retirement to better see to the needs of her grandson and support of his parents, so he knew Ace's situation weighed on her. She nodded briskly to the dish in his hands. "Get that into the freezer now, you hear?"

"Yes, ma'am." He stepped back and bumped into Abby.

"Hello, Janet. Brett's been here painting the garage this week." She snuck that in there as if needing to explain his presence.

He didn't know, though, quite how she planned to explain the drawn shades and the still-flickering candlelight in the room behind them. No matter how Abby couched it, that wouldn't look like garage painting even to a two-year-old.

"That's my boy," Janet said almost proudly, her lips curving into a knowing smile as she turned away to start down the steps. "Give my love to Meg, Abby. And, Brett? Behave yourself."

Back inside, Abby sent Davy upstairs to get cleaned up for bed and his nightly phone call from his mother, then joined Brett in the kitchen, where he'd found a spot for the enchiladas in the freezer. Should he apologize because his presence might have led Janet to make assumptions about the two of them? Or would mentioning it make more of it than it really was and embarrass Abby?

He didn't have to concern himself, though, as she took the conversational reins and steered them in a different direction. "That boy who was at the riding lessons with

Davy and over here tonight—Ace?—Janet's grandson? Did I understand correctly from your conversation that he's not well? I heard him coughing out there when playing Frisbee. Asthma?"

His mind raced to rerun the brief exchange with Janet. Neither of them had actually mentioned Jeremy, had they?

"Cystic fibrosis." He hated naming it aloud. "CF."

Her brow wrinkled as she thought a moment, then shook her head. "I've heard of it, but don't know much about it."

"It's a life-threatening genetic disease that affects the lungs, pancreas and other vital organs." He wouldn't go into any of the heart-wrenching details. She could look it up online herself if she felt so inclined.

"That's why Janet started the summer camp, isn't it? That's the grandson you were talking about that she wanted to make sure enjoyed an authentic outdoor experience."

"It is."

"He's not—" her dark eyes appealed to him for answers "—not going to die from it, is he?"

A muscle tightened in Brett's throat at the compassion in her voice. "He will…eventually. But hopefully not for decades. There are promising treatments—medications— some of which he's on. But no cures."

She momentarily squeezed her eyes shut, as if withdrawing from the imagined horror of it. "I couldn't deal with something like that. Losing a child to an incurable disease."

Well, he had his answer there if he was looking for one. This wasn't a woman who'd want to risk having a child with him.

"But this is terrible," she continued, the soft huskiness of her voice more pronounced. "Why do we never hear about cystic fibrosis?"

He looked away from the outraged demand in her eyes, recognizing it not only from years spent with an angry, grieving Melynda, but from the face that still looked back at him from the mirror at times. "Janet kindheartedly insists it's because those who suffer from it in this country are relatively few, so not as many are impacted by it, like, say, cancer. About thirty thousand people in this country."

"Thirty thousand sounds like a lot to me."

"And to me." He cleared his throat. "I also propose that the search for a cure hasn't drawn big enough celebrity names to champion the funding of it."

"I now see why this summer camp is so important to her."

"It is. It's a place where kids with varying degrees of disability can come and feel, as one enthusiastic participant once put it, 'like a normal kid.' We'd both love to see it expanded so more children can take advantage of it."

"But if you can't find a doctor, it will be canceled this summer, right? Have you had any luck finding one?"

"Not yet, but Janet won't have any choice but to call it off if we don't. It's too risky not to have a physician on-site. Many parents wouldn't consider sending a child with special needs to such a remote location without one."

"And when is this camp again?"

"The last week of June. Just under three weeks away. Why?"

Chapter Nine

Three weeks.

Abby nibbled at her lower lip, hoping Brett wasn't a mind reader. A man who had a sister with the kind of medical experience needed had been trying to get in touch with Abby for over a week. She would hesitate to call Gene's physician sibling directly, though, not knowing how well being contacted by an ex-fiancée she'd only met once would go over. But all Abby had to do was pick up the phone and return Gene's call, ask him to put in a good word with Irene. Most doctors scheduled time off at least six months to a year in advance, but it would be worth a try—if she could bring herself to speak with Gene.

"How long do you have to find a replacement before canceling?"

"Two weeks max, and that's cutting it close. But I'm going to do everything I can to avoid doing that."

Surely he'd find someone soon and she wouldn't feel obligated to help them locate a doctor. She wasn't eager to request a favor from her former fiancé.

The sound of a knock at the back door jerked Abby back into the present.

"Maybe it's another enchilada delivery," Brett quipped, the glint in his eyes that she'd come to associate with him resurfacing. She'd seen a serious side to him tonight that she hadn't expected, yet found the return of the "old" Brett reassuring.

She stepped through the utility room to find her dad on the doorstep holding a foil-covered, lasagna-size pan.

He held it up. "Enchiladas."

She smothered a laugh.

"What's so funny, young lady? Are you going to make me stand out here all night?"

She opened the door wide and her father stepped inside, then moved on into the kitchen.

"Brett." He nodded toward the cowboy as though it were an everyday occurrence to find him there. Then he looked to Abby and lifted the pan. "Sharon made them. One of Joe and Davy's favorites. I'll put it in the freezer for you."

He turned in the direction of the refrigerator, but Brett stepped forward to cut him off as easily as he might have an uncooperative calf. "Let me do that for you, Bill."

"Oh, sure. Thanks."

Dad relinquished the pan and turned back to her while Brett discreetly moved a few things around in the freezer section and secured a spot for it. Mission accomplished, he met her gaze with twinkling eyes.

"Sharon thought Meg might not feel like cooking when she gets back this weekend." Dad spoke as if trying to assure her his girlfriend was a decent sort.

"I'm sure she'll appreciate it. Please tell Sharon thank-you."

"You can tell her yourself. She's out in the truck."

"You left her sitting in the truck?" Did Sharon sense she and Dad needed one-on-one time and opted to remain behind while Dad came to the door? Or had Dad bluntly told her his daughter was uncomfortable with them as a couple? She hoped not. Her feelings had nothing to do with Sharon personally.

"When she saw Brett's vehicle, she didn't want to intrude. I told her he's just here to paint the garage." He glanced over at Brett. "How's that coming?"

"It's still too breezy to apply the primer."

Breezy. That's what folks in the Arizona high country called thirty- and forty-mile-per-hour winds.

"Better get it done before the pine pollen shakes loose. Could be any day now." He focused again on Abby. "You may not remember from when you were a kid, but that ponderosa pollen billows through the trees in slow-moving waves, almost like clouds of smoke. Coats everything it comes in contact with."

She shook her head. As much as she remembered from childhood in Canyon Springs, there were so many things that had slipped away. Either evaporated entirely or remained fuzzy.

Brett chuckled. "Bryce Harding says newcomers to the area get spooked and call the fire department."

"I imagine he'd rather have them call," she said in defense of the tourists, "than have it be real smoke and ignored."

"True," Brett acknowledged as he moved in the direction of the living room. "I'll retrieve my hat and boots and let myself out. I have a few phone calls to make on behalf of the kids' camp. Thanks for supper, Abby. I'll see you at noon tomorrow."

When he disappeared, her father peered over the top of his glasses. "He joined you for supper? And what's with the noonish thing tomorrow?"

Telltale warmth crept into her cheeks. Brett's presence had been a totally innocent circumstance, but Dad's expression and the tone of his query intimated it had been something more. "He came by to play Frisbee with Davy and the dogs tonight and Davy invited him to supper.

When school lets out tomorrow, he's taking Davy to buy Western-wear."

Dad nodded knowingly. "That's as good of an excuse as any to drop in and see my beautiful daughter. I guess Sharon wasn't far off the mark, was she? Nice young man, that Brett. A regular Boy Scout. Maybe I'll have to slip him a little something on the side if he can persuade you to stick around."

"Don't you dare."

"You're not chasing this one off like you did the last one, are you?"

"Believe me," she evaded, "Gene Daymert was no Boy Scout." Yet here she was, debating whether or not to ask him to persuade his physician sister to come to Canyon Springs for a week.

"No, maybe not. But while you might find Brett on the high-spirited side, he's building his life on a solid foundation as far as I can see. Hard worker. Comes from good family I'm told. Makes God a big part of his life. Loves kids."

That again.

"I won't be in town but a few more days."

Dad was silent a long moment, staring down at the floor, then he again focused on her. "And why is that, Abby? You show up here out of the blue, get all our hopes up and then can't get out of town fast enough."

She got all *their* hopes up? What about hers?

"It's not…" How could she explain it without hurting his feelings even more than she'd probably already hurt them?

"You mean it's not like it was when you were a kid," he filled in. "Between you and me, you mean."

When he stated it like that, it made her feel immature. On the drive from Tucson she'd reminded herself that things would be different and it would take time to rebuild relationships long dormant. Head knowledge told her they'd need time to establish a new connection as adults. Mom had warned to guard her expectations, so she thought she'd been as prepared as possible to deal with whatever reality turned out to be.

But she hadn't expected reality to be so awkward, so disappointing. Despite steeling herself to face whatever the situation might call for, she'd allowed herself to dream of pulling up in front of her father's place and running into his open arms as she'd done so many times as a child.

Daddy! Daddy!

But she hadn't even been able to bring herself to tell him about her inability to bear children. When they'd come face-to-face upon her arrival, she'd realized she couldn't turn to her father for comfort, for answers. The realization that he could no longer kiss it and make it all better as he'd done when she'd been a child raised an invisible barrier between them.

She took a deep breath. "No, it's not working. Not like I thought—hoped—it would."

"So you pack up and go back to Tucson. That's it. Done deal."

"Too much time has passed. Maybe it would have been different if you'd have invited me and Ed up to spend occasional holidays or summers with you."

His brows lowered and she knew she'd done it again. Laid the blame at his feet.

"I did invite you. But your mother thought it would be too disruptive and would make it all the harder for you both to settle back into your life down there with her."

A muscle in her throat tightened. Mom had never said a word about that. Was it the truth or was Dad trying to justify himself and didn't think she'd dare ask Mom about it for fear of opening up old wounds? She made a restless motion. "We shouldn't leave Sharon sitting in the truck by herself. I'll go out and thank her for the enchiladas."

"No need. I'll relay the message."

He moved to the back door, but she followed close behind and brought him to a halt with a light touch to his arm.

"Dad, you say you want me to stay in Canyon Springs for a while. You've even intimated you'd like me to relocate here. But what's the point? I don't know what else to do to make it right between us. Do you?"

They gazed into each other's eyes, a heaviness settling deeper and deeper into Abby's heart with every second he didn't respond, didn't offer the answers she needed to hear. Answers she hungered for.

He shook his head in apparent resignation and stepped into the twilight.

"So, care to share when we're going to meet her?" Brett's sister Geri inquired as they wrapped up their phone conversation Wednesday morning. Early mornings were best for both of them to touch base. For him before he had to head off to work and for her before the kids woke up.

"Meet who?"

"This Abby person. I don't think I've heard you mention a woman's name in seven years of phone calls as many times as you've slipped hers into this one."

Had he? Naw. As usual, his sister was exaggerating. How many times through the years had she pounced on the name of any female he mentioned and tried to read something into it?

"As I already said, we go to the same church and I'm painting her brother's garage." Geri didn't need to know they'd be going shopping together that afternoon. "So yeah, I see her occasionally."

Coffee mug in hand, Brett sat in one of the front porch rocking chairs at his cabin, watching the sun rise through a gap in the trees. Chilly morning. He leaned over to scratch Elmo behind the ears.

"When did you start that painting? You're usually fast with those projects. Maybe *someone* is dragging his feet in order to spend more time with this Abby?"

"I can't paint when it's windy. Too much debris in the air. Besides, she's only a visitor from Tucson who's here for the week."

"*Only* a visitor? Come on, Brett. Who are you trying to kid? Your voice lit up like a kid's when you told me about that banana with legs, her expertise at Bible storytelling and the clever distraction the flameless candles provided her nephew. You worked her into the conversation in any way you could find. There's no harm in admitting you like someone."

He sat back in the rocker and took a sip of coffee. "I can admit I like her. She's a nice gal."

"Seems to me you think she's more than nice. Just because she goes back home, it doesn't mean things have to end. How far is it to Tucson from there anyway? A four-hour drive or something like that? People meet online and court long-distance all the time. How much better that the two of you have already met and are getting to know each other."

"Geri, you and the rest of my matchmaking family always seem to forget one major factor."

She gave an exasperated sigh. "Cystic fibrosis."

"Right. It's no minor thing."

"I know that. I know there's no cure yet. But strides are being made in research. Didn't you once tell me that the average CF patient can live well into their thirties now? Maybe to forty or longer?"

"That's an average, which means a bunch of people don't make it that far. Even in their twenties they might be lugging canisters of oxygen around wherever they go, hoping and praying they live long enough for a lung transplant. Jeremy also had complications from CF that put him on the low end of the survival stats."

"Abby may not even be a CF carrier. She probably isn't."

Brett stood, then moved to lean against a support post and gaze up at the silhouetted ponderosas.

"But she could be. I've seen it suggested that one out of every thirty or so white Americans may have the defective gene. Maybe one out of sixty-five African-Americans. That's not odds I care to play around with." But how was he to find that out before he fell in love with a woman and she with him? *Pardon me, ma'am, but let's not get too attached to each other until you take a test that will put my mind at ease.*

"I realize that," his sister persisted, "but even if she turned out to be a carrier, you and this Abby would have a 75 percent chance of *not* having a child with CF. Right?"

His jaw tightened as the unwelcome vision of a pregnant Abby flashed through his mind. *You can tell,* Davy's childish voice reminded, *because the moms get real big.* He squeezed his eyes tight to banish the image. He didn't want to think about having a baby with Abby Diaz. He hardly knew the woman. "Look, Geri—"

"Even if you and this Abby or some other woman did have a child with CF, think how much longer they'd be likely to live."

As her words sliced through him, he pushed roughly away from the support post and strode to the far side of the porch, Elmo at his heels. He couldn't believe his sister had the nerve to say that. Managing to hold his anger in check, his response nevertheless came out more gruff than intended.

"Do you think it would be any easier to see a grown-up Jeremy suffer? Be any easier to lose a child you'd come to know and love as an adult than it was to say goodbye when he was five?"

That silenced her.

"No," she said after a long moment, her voice now subdued. "Of course not. I'm sorry."

He ran his free hand roughly through his hair. She was trying to help him look at things in a positive light. "It's okay. Don't worry about it. I'm sensitive about this."

"You have every reason to be. I was being *in*sensitive."

He let out a heavy gust of breath and set his coffee mug on the porch railing. "There aren't any easy answers to this. You know how much I still want to have kids, but do I trust God that a woman I fall in love with isn't a carrier? Or do I take steps to ensure that she isn't?"

"I know it's hard."

That was an understatement.

"Do I trust God that if she is a carrier, too, and we have children, that the child won't have CF? Or do we decide not to have kids at all?" Anguish tore the words from the depths of his heart. "Would that decision mean we'd be saying that if a child is born less than perfect and we can only have them in our life a short while that we don't want them here at all? That we can't love them and be loved by them because it causes us too much pain?"

Brett pressed his lips together, stemming any further outburst. Life wouldn't have been the same without Jeremy, his precious gift from God.

"I'm sorry. I know you've lived with these kinds of questions every day since Jeremy was diagnosed."

He hadn't only lived with them, he'd been tormented by them at times, relief only coming when he reminded himself that God was in control. That God loved him and God loved Jeremy. That he didn't have to fear tomorrow because God was already there.

Life had been relatively peaceful for the most part the past several years. He'd thought he'd come to terms with the possibility he might be called to a life of childlessness.

Maybe even singleness. But the past few days, time and time again the issues, the haunting questions he'd thought he'd laid to rest, again reared their ugly heads.

And he knew why.

He'd awakened that morning with the realization that it had all started when Abby Diaz walked into the arena at the High Country Equine Center.

Chapter Ten

She hadn't heard Brett's truck after all.

"Where is he, Aunt Abby?" Davy eagerly paced the front porch as he'd been doing for the past fifty minutes.

With the toe of her sandaled foot, she halted the rock of the porch swing where she'd been sitting. "Something probably came up at work that delayed him."

"Like horses got loose or something?"

"Maybe." The least Brett could do, though, was call. It was almost one o'clock and neither she nor Davy had eaten yet because Brett said they'd catch lunch in Show Low. She hadn't thought to exchange cell phone numbers with him, but he could call Joe's landline.

She gave her nephew an encouraging smile, her heart going out to him. This situation felt all too familiar. How many times growing up had she eagerly anticipated her mother's arrival to take her to piano lessons or a birthday party, to come watch her in a spelling bee or view her science fair project—only to have Mom forget?

Should she give Brett the benefit of the doubt? Last night he said he'd see her tomorrow. Surely he wouldn't forget Davy so easily, would he? Then again, except for the glimpse she'd had of a more serious side when he'd talked about Ace's health issues, he seemed fairly casual in his dealings with life in general. He didn't even hold down a regular job, but rather part-time ones in addition to handyman assignments. He always seemed more than ready to laugh and flirt, a good-time-guy from a big happy family who hadn't known a heartache in his whole life.

She didn't have more than a casual interest in Brett, of course, but hadn't Mina Ricks warned that if she happened to be looking for a keeper, to steer clear of the charming cowboy? Maybe this was why. And to think she'd primped to the max for a guy like that. What had gotten into her? For all his faults, at least Gene had been reliable—right up until the abrupt end of their relationship anyway.

Davy plopped down on the porch steps, elbows on his knees and his chin propped in his hands. Should she call the equine center to see if she could track down Brett? She couldn't bear to see her nephew disappointed. She'd been there too many times herself to wish that on any child and still remembered the sick feeling in her tummy and the ache in her throat when she'd tried not to cry.

Was it any wonder she'd become such a punctual, on-the-dot type person? Perhaps too rigid in some of her choices? Even her conservative preference of dress was, she could admit, an effort to distance herself from her mother's flamboyant style.

"Are you getting hungry, Davy? I am. I'll fix us sandwiches while we wait."

"Brett said we'd have pizza."

"I know, but even if we leave right now it will be later in the afternoon by the time we get there." She rose from the porch swing. "I'm starving and I imagine you are, too."

He reluctantly nodded, as if agreeing somehow betrayed his cowboy friend. "Fix a sandwich for Brett, too, okay? We don't want him to starve, either."

That's right. Brett was *always* hungry.

"I will." She headed inside to the kitchen, intending

to do as Davy requested. But Brett better have a good excuse for standing up a little boy.

Brett knew the minute Abby came to the door that he was in hot water. Or rather, the deep freeze. Her body language registered eighty degrees cooler than it was where he stood on the front porch. Not even a hint of a welcoming smile.

"Brett! I knew you'd come." Davy pushed past Abby and opened the screen door wide. Then he drew back, his nose wrinkling. "You stink."

"I guess I do." He couldn't deny that candid assessment. He probably looked as bad as he smelled, too, but Abby didn't appear inclined to cut him any slack. Sensing a more forgiving welcome from her nephew, he focused on the boy.

"I'm sorry I didn't make our shopping trip, Davy."

"Can we go *now?*"

"It's too late for that tonight. I've got to get cleaned up and get back to work. But we'll reschedule and get 'er done."

"Tomorrow?" Davy looked hopefully at his aunt Abby.

"We'll see," she said, not making any promises.

Davy motioned to him. "Don't leave yet, Brett. We have something for you."

Brett stomped his feet as if rooting himself to the ground. "I'll stay right here."

The boy dashed off, and only then did Brett dare to once again meet Abby's cool stare.

"We wondered what had happened to you."

She didn't invite him in. Not that he'd take her up on her offer as grungy as he was at the moment, but it told him where he stood. She had every right to be ticked off. When he realized he'd left his cell phone behind in a jacket pocket, he should have thought to borrow Trey's phone. But the unvarnished truth was that he had a one-track mind and hadn't even thought of Davy. Not once.

It was hard to build an airtight defense for that.

"A neighbor's pasture caught fire about five miles north of Duffy's when someone's tire blew out on the highway next to it. We haven't had any moisture since April, so it's like a tinderbox. The wind routed the wildfire toward a barn and timber, so it was all hands on deck to catch spooked horses and trailer them and get a fortune in hay out of harm's way."

"I'm sorry to hear that," Abby said under her breath. "But you couldn't have called? Davy sat on the front porch all afternoon, sure you'd show up. He finally came inside a short while ago when I lured him in with cookies. I called the equine center several times this afternoon, but no one answered. We started to get worried."

She'd been worried about him? So this cold shoulder was about more than disappointing Davy?

"I'm sorry, Abby. We left our teenage summer hires to watch over the property, but I guess they weren't manning phones while Trey and I lent a hand to corral the fire."

"I see."

"We got the call about forty minutes before I was to meet you and, quite honestly, I'd left my cell phone back at Duffy's and didn't so much as think about our planned excursion until—" he glanced at his watch, almost four o'clock "—about twenty minutes ago. I came straight here."

"Is the fire out now? Was anyone hurt?"

All business. He hated letting a kid down, but he'd make it up to him. And her.

"Pretty much out. It didn't get too far into the timber, but despite fire trucks from several surrounding communities, it was touch and go for a while. They'll watch it tonight for flare-ups. No one was hurt."

"Brett!" Davy again joined them at the door, holding out something plastic-wrapped. "It's sandwiches Aunt Abby made for you. You can have chips and a cookie, too."

He reached for the offering as his gaze flicked to hers with what he hoped was fitting contriteness. "I didn't expect a meal."

He ventured a smile, which she didn't return.

"It's hardly a meal. When we didn't hear from you, I knew Davy needed to eat something. He insisted we not forget you."

Even though *he'd* forgotten *them*. Her implication was clear.

No doubt about it, he had major amends to make.

Davy moved in closer. "So you had a fire, Brett? Cool. I wish I could have seen it. We didn't see or smell smoke here."

"A fire like that isn't cool, Davy. It's dangerous." Kind of how Abby looked at the moment. "The wind was blowing away from town, so that's probably why you weren't aware of it."

Abby had said she was worried about him. Would she have been even more concerned had she seen smoke clouds billowing into the sky? For some reason the possibility that she might be touched his heart.

She hadn't yet said when they could reschedule Davy's shopping trip, but that might be better left to a later conversation. It probably wouldn't be a good time to share his cell number with her, either, not that it would have done any good today since he hadn't had it with him.

"Well, I guess I'd better be moseying along...." She didn't make any effort to stop him. "I need to get myself cleaned up so I can get back to Duffy's tonight. I'll freak out the horses if I stink as bad as Davy says I do."

"You do."

Was that a twinge of a smile? For a moment he was

tempted to follow up on it, to see if he could provoke a bigger one. Maybe even a laugh. But he'd better not push his luck.

She shouldn't have been so hard on Brett.

Abby had tossed and turned all night, knowing she owed him an apology. He had a perfectly legitimate reason for having forgotten her and Davy. Wildfires were nothing to mess with in the drought-ridden regions of Arizona, especially in the forested mountains where it wasn't unheard of to lose hundreds of thousands of acres of pristine timber to a campfire improperly put out. Being a good neighbor in an emergency was expected in these parts.

She'd apologize to him, although that wouldn't make up for jumping to conclusions that he was like her mother. She had to admit, too, that as the hours stretched and he didn't show up yesterday, her anger had faded as she'd become concerned about him.

Yes, she owed him an apology. But when? He probably wasn't in any hurry to see *her* again.

"Good coffee, sis." Joe placed his mug on the glass-topped table as she stepped out the French doors to join him on the patio. Joe had gotten home before supper last evening, much to Davy's delight, and intended to spend time with his son before heading off for another shift midafternoon.

"Dad says you're planning to go back to Tucson as soon as Meg gets home." Joe's dark eyes studied her as she pulled out a chair and sat down.

So Joe and Dad had been talking about her.

"I promise to come back for a visit after the baby's born." Maybe when Jori got out of diapers—or graduated from high school. "I've enjoyed getting to know Davy. And of course, spending time with Meg last week. But…"

"But coming back to Canyon Springs isn't what you'd

hoped it would be. That's partly my fault. I've been gone so much since you got here."

She made a dismissive motion. "You're a responsible husband and father and a busy paramedic. I don't expect your whole world to grind to a halt to accommodate me."

"No, but when you showed up last week it wasn't my plan to jump at the opportunity to stick you with Davy and then disappear."

"I don't feel like I've been stuck with Davy." Not much anyway. She was getting used to him and he to her. Her thoughts didn't often wander to aching for a boy just like him. But a pregnant woman or newborn in the house…? That would be a different story. "What happened with Meg and the baby couldn't be helped."

Joe took another sip of coffee, then leaned forward. "I realize you have a life elsewhere, but I wish you'd reconsider staying. I think Dad's desperate, even pinning his hopes on Brett Marden to get you to stick around."

She pushed back in her chair. "What are you talking about?"

"He says Brett's been hanging around here, keeping you company."

"He's not been keeping me company." She folded her arms. "You're the one who hired him to paint your garage and he came over to play Frisbee with Davy when *you* had to work. You're the one who okayed him to take your son shopping for Western-wear and I would have been dragged into it."

"Whoa." Joe held up a hand in protest. "Easy there."

"You and Dad can get those silly notions out of your head. Come on, Joe, stop and think. The man is a *cowboy*." A good-looking one, too, but that was beside the point. "Do I look like cowgirl material to you?"

"Okay, okay. But Dad wants you to spend the summer here at home. What would it hurt?"

"This isn't home anymore. Not for me anyway. Besides, I need to snag a job and get started back on my coursework." A doctorate was on her radar, but she'd cut back on classes last year to spend more time with Gene. Dumb move. Then this year she hadn't been up to registering for the first summer session. Whoever would have anticipated the demoralizing impact of a broken engagement and the shattering of a long-held dream of motherhood? The layoff compounded that lethargy.

"What's another few weeks? Dad's not been himself since you came back."

"That makes me feel good." She took a steadying breath, not wanting to bicker with Joe as they had when they were kids. Funny how she remembered that now when for years she'd painted a rosy glow around their real-life brother-sister relationship.

"Dad wants to make things good between the two of you, but he's not sure how to do that, so give him a break."

"We both all but admitted a few nights ago that we're making each other miserable. We had a decent long-distance relationship. But the in-person stuff isn't working. We either can't think of anything to say to each other or we rub each other wrong. Those aren't memories to cherish. It's better to go back to the way it was, letting our imaginations fill in the gaps and convincing ourselves we have a normal father-daughter relationship."

Joe toyed with the handle of his coffee mug. "I realize you and I see different sides to our parents' story. You've had mom's perspective for eighteen years and I've had Dad's. But you forget, when Mom took off with you and Ed and left him behind, she left me, too."

Her brother felt he'd been abandoned? She'd never given that much thought. But of course he would have. He'd been the only child out of the three she hadn't taken with her. Abby had always assumed he'd chosen to stay with Dad.

"You probably aren't even aware of this, Abby—I wasn't until a short time ago because he never talked about it—but Dad blamed himself for not being who Mom needed him to be, so he stood silent when she walked out the door. He came to deeply regret not going after her and telling her how much he loved her and doing anything within his power to make things work—even leaving his beloved Canyon Springs. In fact, at a point when I came close to losing Meg, it was Dad who spurred me on not to make the same mistakes he had."

"You almost lost Meg?" That was unthinkable. From what she'd seen, they were perfect for each other.

"It was a close call."

"Mom and Dad weren't a match made in Heaven like you and Meg are."

Joe gazed across the treed backyard. "Believe me, even many matches that appear on the surface to be made in Heaven have been forged in the fire of day-to-day life right here on earth. Through putting the thirteenth chapter of the first book of Corinthians into daily practice."

Ah, yes. The love-never-fails chapter of the Bible that clarified genuine love is far from hormones on fire or starry-eyed feelings. She didn't know much about that higher level of love when it came to the male-female realm. Mom and Dad hadn't pulled it off and Gene hadn't made any effort in that direction. She doubted Brett Marden knew much about it, either.

"That Scripture is often cited at weddings," Joe continued, "but in context it's not about marriages, it's about relationships in general, including the one between fathers and daughters."

Irritation rippled.

"So you're saying that by leaving now I'm not being patient? Kind? That I'm keeping a record of wrongs? Not persevering?"

"Look, I know what I'm talking about. When I moved back here, Dad and I were in the same place the two of you are now." He shrugged. "So if the shoe fits…"

Dad and now Joe. She was the one who'd made the effort to come here in the first place. Where had they been all these years? Not reaching out to her and Ed, that was for certain.

"To be quite honest, a lot of things have happened to me in the past six months that have left me drained and not much up to a challenge like this." She wanted to go home and forget about her misguided journey to Canyon Springs. Forget about the twinkly-eyed cowboy whose smile set her heart dancing. "The timing is all wrong."

Joe stood and reached for his coffee mug, pausing to look squarely down at her. "When will it ever be right, Abby?"

Chapter Eleven

Brett hadn't expected to find Abby at the secondhand shop. From the car she drove to the name-brand clothes she wore, she didn't seem the type to find treasures among the castaways of others. But there she was, the source of so much of his recent heartache, stirring up inner turmoil he'd thought he'd laid to rest.

She knelt next to an armless, painted rocker badly in need of refinishing, a crease of concentration between her brows as she inspected the piece. She hadn't spied him yet. He could slip out easily enough and she'd be none the wiser that he'd skedaddled back to Duffy's. But against his better judgment, he found himself slowly making his way in her direction, breathing in the store's dry, musty odor as he wove between the shabby chic furnishings his mom and sisters delighted in. A floorboard creaked under his booted foot as he neared and, startled, Abby looked up.

"You're a secondhand shopper, too?" She stood to brush off her calf-length skirt, giving him an uneasy look. Maybe she was trying to decide if she should belt him for forgetting about her and Davy.

"You can find some good stuff here if you keep your eyes open. Like that rocker." In fact, it was the same rocker he'd spotted a few days ago, but hadn't made up his mind about. You snooze, you lose, Geri would admonish, especially when it came to the women passing through his life. Like Abby.

"There's a rocker in the baby's room, but not downstairs. I thought this one might fit nicely in the living room, where Meg could look out a window. She'd like the carved motif, too."

A tiny heart.

He squatted by the rocker and ran his hand along the back, then peeled off a small strip of the dried-out paint to study the wood grain. "I can't tell for sure, but it may possibly be oak. As old as the paint is, though, it's slightly discolored the wood."

Abby leaned closer to look, the sweet scent of her filling his senses.

"I'll take your word for it that it's oak. But the red lacquer definitely has to go. Why would someone paint a rocker with such beautiful lines such a gaudy color and cover up the wood?"

"It could be damaged underneath."

Her forehead crinkled. "I didn't think of that."

"It could be they wanted to put it outside and didn't want the elements to warp it. Or maybe they were crazy people who painted all their furniture red."

She laughed, the worry lines evaporating, and his heart lifted. Apparently he was a hopeless case when it came to Abby Diaz and that rare, dazzling smile of hers. If only he didn't have to fight the attraction and could be free to pursue her. But in spite of his sister's encouragement, he couldn't figure out a way to get around reality.

"So where's Davy?" With school out, he figured she'd have a willing shadow.

"With his dad. He and Joe went fishing at Casey Lake."

"You didn't jump at the chance to go along and thread a few worms or fluorescent goop on a hook?"

She laughed again. He could get used to this.

"Actually, Dad used to take us fishing when we were kids. I loved it." A woman who loved fishing? Abby was looking better and better. "But this morning I needed time to myself and I thought Davy needed time alone with his dad."

She again ran an assessing gaze over the rocker. "I do like this and I think Meg will, too, once it's cleaned up. You've done quite a bit of this? Refinishing, I mean?"

"Whenever I can. It's relaxing. Your hands are busy but your mind can wander. I like to think about how God's in the process of sanding down the remaining evidence of our old damaged selves, bringing out the core, eternal beauty He placed inside us when we gave our lives to Him."

"Wow. That's deep."

She sounded surprised, not realizing cowboys tending to herds, horses and property had time to commune with nature and God if they'd so choose. Kind of like that shepherd boy, David. Yes, time to think deep thoughts. Melynda had made fun of him when he'd shared some of his with her. But by that point she couldn't understand why he was on speaking terms with God anyway, what with how things were going with Jeremy.

He gave the rocker a push to set it in motion. "What about you? Are you an old hand at this?"

She shook her head as she gazed doubtfully at the chipped, glossy paint. "Total amateur. Is it something you think I can manage? Something I can get done by the time Meg arrives home and I have to leave?"

"I don't see any reason why not if you get right on it. I'd be happy to give you some tips. Lend a hand even." Her eyes narrowed slightly, as if undecided at the latter offer, but helping out could make retribution for having stood her and Davy up. "Maybe I can find a table to go with it. We could match the finishes."

Her eyes brightened. "Like a set? Meg would love that. Their living room furniture is medium oak, so that might be a good choice."

He stood to gaze around the clutter of furniture, then swiftly wove his way to the far side of the room to a white-painted table about two and a half feet tall. Topped by a twelve-by-twelve square, it featured a drawer and an open shelf beneath it.

"What do you think of this?" he called, holding it up for her to see. "It might not be big enough for a lamp, but it would hold a cup of tea. A book might fit in the drawer."

"I like it."

"Finding what you're looking for?" A snowy-haired gentleman Brett recognized as the owner had stepped to the doorway behind Abby.

"I think we have, Lester." Brett hoisted the table above his head and negotiated his way back to where Abby stood. Then he placed it next to the rocker. "What do you think, Abby?"

"If the finishes can be harmonized, looks like a match. The table even has a heart-shaped drawer pull."

The older man shuffled over to them, hands in his pockets. "You're a smart couple not to invest in a lot of new furnishings until you see how your tastes meld. The old stuff was made better anyway. If you get this thing refinished, fifty years from now you could be rocking your grandbabies in it."

Abby's gaze met Brett's in clear discomfort.

He smiled at the well-meaning man. "You're getting ahead of yourself there, Les. I'm helping a lady who's visiting town to pick out a few pieces intended for a gift."

The store owner grimaced, then chuckled. "Oh, sorry. My apologies. You looked like you went together." Did they? A guy in a cowboy hat and boots and a woman who looked like she stepped off the pages of some fashion magazine? "I guess I shouldn't jump to conclusions, should I?"

"I don't mind you thinking I could go with her," Brett teased, attempting to catch Abby's eye, "but I have a feeling she might not want you to think she goes with me."

The man laughed. "So that's how it is, is it?"

Brett cast another look at Abby, who quickly turned away. Then he picked up the rocker with one hand and the table with the other. "I think we've both found what we came for."

"Then let's get you checked out, shall we?"

Once everything was paid for, Brett carried the pieces outside the store, where Abby drew to a halt.

"Oh, no."

"What?"

She turned to him in obvious embarrassment. "It was such a beautiful morning that I went for a walk and ended up here. I didn't come intending to buy anything."

His heart still strangely warmed that the secondhand shop owner believed he and Abby to be a couple, he motioned to his Ford parked across Main Street and a few businesses farther down the way. "That's what pickups are for."

"Do you have time? I can come back for it or Joe can."

"It's no problem. I have time."

Walking along in front of the shops with Abby at his side was sweeter than he'd have imagined. He nodded to a couple of folks he knew, noting with satisfaction their evident curiosity as to who his lady friend might be. Funny, but it seemed people looked at him more respectfully when they thought he might have such a classy-looking gal friend.

But he didn't pause to chat as he might have any other day.

He had only this midday break and, for reasons he

didn't care to analyze, he selfishly wanted to keep Abby to himself for as long as he could.

Abby cringed inwardly. How silly to have bought something without even thinking about how she'd get it home. Brett probably thought her a total airhead. But she'd have better thought out the purchase if he hadn't shown up and distracted her. All she could think of was apologizing to him for yesterday's behavior.

At the truck, he let down the tailgate and spread a tarp across the bed. Then he wrapped the rocker and table in a couple of woven, gaily colored Mexican blankets so they wouldn't slide around.

He turned to her. "So, where are you planning to work on the rocker? Joe's place? Or your dad's?"

She grimaced. Another strike against her. "I hadn't thought that far ahead. Refinishing furniture probably isn't something you do in the living room, is it? How much of a mess will it make?"

"When that thick coat of red starts to dissolve, it could get ugly. You might want to do this outside, with something underneath it for protection. I have some old boxes I can break down to serve as a base, then you'd layer newspapers on top of that. Once the red's off you'll be okay to work on it in the garage if you spread out newspapers or a tarp."

"What else do I need to buy? Paint remover? Brushes?" Hopefully nothing too expensive.

"Not a thing. Last fall I refinished a couple of chairs for my mom, so I have everything you need. Even the medium oak finish you described. If you want, we can swing by Singing Rock to pick up everything on the way."

"Are you sure you have time to do this? You can drop me off at Joe's if you want, and I can get the other things later."

"I imagine you'd like to get started on the rocker this afternoon, wouldn't you?"

"That would be nice." She had no idea how long something like this took, but the weekend was fast approaching.

"Then let's do it." Brett opened the truck's passenger-side door and helped Abby into the cab, then strode to the other side and climbed in.

"Over the river and through the woods—" he sang in an exaggerated baritone once he'd slammed the door "—to Singing Rock now we go."

She couldn't help but laugh. It was getting to be a habit around him.

He backed the truck, then they headed down Main Street and on out to the highway. She partially rolled down her window, the beat of a country-and-western tune playing softly on the radio as she mentally rehearsed the words she knew she had to say.

On the outskirts of town, she clasped her hands in her lap. "I owe you an apology for yesterday."

Brett cast her a questioning glance.

"You know, for the way I wasn't very nice when you came to apologize to Davy. I was pretty ugly."

"You? Ugly, pretty lady? Never." Brett chuckled, then tipped his head toward her. "Although I did feel a well-deserved temperature drop when you opened the door. But you had every right to be irritated with me."

She lightly touched his arm. "I might have had a reason, but I didn't have a right."

"I let Davy down in a major way. You, too."

"But you didn't do it intentionally. You couldn't help that there was an emergency and you didn't have your cell phone with you. When you didn't show up—"

"You got worried?"

"Yes," she admitted grudgingly, "but that's not why I behaved the way I did when you finally showed up."

"Care to share?" He raised a brow. "That's what my sister Geri is always asking me. Drives me crazy, so you can ignore it if you want to."

"No, I need to come clean." She closed her eyes momentarily, letting the breeze coming through the partially open window cool her cheeks and flutter her hair. Then she turned to him again. "Being late or not showing up at all is so typical of my mom."

"Ah." He glanced in the rearview mirror, then focused again on the road. "So I pushed the wrong buttons."

"Yeah, you did. Don't get me wrong, I love my mother. She's wonderful. So much fun. But when you didn't show up, didn't call, it dredged up a bunch of bad memories. That's what I took out on you."

"So your mom isn't always reliable?"

"I can't tell you how many times as a kid I was the last one to be picked up. Those in charge of the events had their own plans messed up, all because of Mom. It was humiliating. By the time I graduated from middle school, I'd gravitated to activities that didn't involve depending on her. There wasn't much that could be goofed up if you're involved in solitary pursuits."

"But you said you took riding lessons starting in middle school. How'd you get to and from them?"

"Bus. Then my brother when he learned to drive." She caught Brett's frown. "I'm sure this is more information than you wanted, but you deserve to know that how I acted yesterday wasn't your fault. It was mine."

He kept his eyes on the road, but nodded thoughtfully. "Thanks for telling me. I appreciate it."

Exhaling a relieved breath, she shook back her hair and poked him playfully in the arm. "I guess you won't ask me if I'll 'care to share' again, will you, cowboy?"

He gave her a lopsided grin. "I don't know about that.

I like learning more about you, Abby Diaz. I'm just sorry that my messing up yesterday stirred all that up for you."

She lifted a shoulder, dismissing his apology. "Well, that's the reality of Mom and me. If what happened yesterday afternoon hadn't forced me to explain today, I'm not sure I'd be beginning to recognize the truth."

"The truth of what?"

"The truth of how hard things must have been on Dad being married to Mom. She grew up in Philadelphia and met Dad when she was doing an internship in Virginia and he was in the navy. They moved here when he got out, but there was nowhere to put her degree to use and she never adjusted to small-town life." Abby let out a sigh. "I think she tried, though. But while she might not be the most reliable mother on the planet at times, at least she never walked off and abandoned me like she did Dad and Joe."

Brett's hands tightened on the steering wheel as he slowed for a turn, his words coming carefully. "I knew your folks had split, but I hadn't realized that's what happened."

"Joe says Dad regretted letting her go, that he blamed himself. But from what I know of Mom's side of it, I don't think there's anything he could have done to stop her. It wasn't his fault."

Brett braked at the rustic sign announcing Singing Rock Cabin Resort and turned onto the gravel road through the pines.

"Maybe," Brett said softly as he headed the truck down the winding road, "you should let your dad know that."

Chapter Twelve

What he wouldn't give to hear God tell him Melynda's departure wasn't his fault, that he'd done everything a man could do to make things right between them, to honor his vows.

It sounded as if Bill had lived with that burden a long, long time. But the Diaz family situation explained a lot about who Abby was now. No wonder she'd grown up overly conscientious, more of an observer of life in some ways than a participant. It seemed, too, that he and Bill had more in common than he'd been aware of—not a mutually agreed upon split with a spouse, but a wife who'd walked away and didn't look back.

Interesting that even though Abby and her dad weren't finding a lot of common ground right now, she'd come to the conclusion that the divorce didn't lay entirely at his feet. He hoped she'd tell her dad that. Sometimes a man needed to hear he'd done all he could.

The route to Singing Rock was every bit as beautiful as it ever was, maybe more so with Abby sitting beside him. With the windows rolled down, they drove along slowly under the shady arch of trees, gravel crunching under the pickup's tires, lost in their own thoughts. When they crossed the bridge over the creek the property was named after and came into a clearing, Abby pointed to a cabin slightly set back in the trees.

"That's where my aunt Rosa and uncle Paul live, right?"

"It is." He'd forgotten Bill and Paul were brothers. He motioned to the two-story lodge opposite it. "And your cousin Olivia lives there in a second-floor apartment."

She gazed around as if trying to orient herself. "This all seems so weird. I remember coming here when I was a kid. It's the same and yet different. And to think Olivia is married to Meg's brother now and they're running Singing Rock. Canyon Springs is like a big puzzle with so many pieces to put back together."

"I'm sure it seems strange after being gone so long."

"It does. So you live in one of the cabins?"

"I'll show you." He drove past the lodge and, instead of taking the looping road through the property that led to dozens of secluded log dwellings, he swung in the opposite direction and pulled up in front of a cabin not far from the main lodge. Elmo must have heard the truck as from behind the house his bark welcomed them home.

Abby sat up straighter, eagerly examining the deep front porch, the native stone chimney and a half barrel of petunias by the steps. "You know, I think I remember playing in this one at a family get-together. It was like an oversize dollhouse."

"It's tiny all right." But it was all he needed. He wasn't much for big empty indoor spaces that had to be cleaned and filled with furniture you seldom used. It suited him just fine.

He reached for the door latch. "I need to pick up another pair of work gloves. I tore a hole through mine this morning. Give me another minute and I'll get the stuff you'll need for the rocker, too."

"Your place sure is cute. I'm sure it's the one I played in as a kid."

He could take a hint. "Do you want to see inside?"

"May I?"

His mind raced ahead, trying to remember in what condition he'd left the place that morning. Had he made the bed? Washed up the dishes? "Sure."

She popped her door open and jumped out.

Then it hit him.

"Hang on a sec, okay? Let me make sure nothing life-endangering has crept out from under the sofa while I've been gone."

"You forget," she teased. "I have two brothers. I don't expect *Better Homes and Gardens*."

"Come on, give this old bachelor a break."

She laughed. "Okay. I'll count to ten, then ready or not, here I come."

He wagged a warning finger at her, liking this playful side of Abby. "Count to twenty—slowly—and we'll have a deal."

"Okay." She climbed back into the truck cab and folded her arms. "One…"

Man, that was close. He dashed to the cabin and up the porch steps. Inside he headed straight for the fireplace mantel and plucked up half a dozen framed photos, then paused to gaze down at them.

His boy smiled back at him and guilt stabbed at what he was about to do. Abby probably wouldn't notice the cowboy-hatted youngster and his pony among the clutter of photos.

But she might.

Although he himself saw a lot of Melynda in their boy, he'd often been told how much father and son resembled each other.

"Here I come," Abby called a warning. The truck door slammed.

"Forgive me, Jeremy," he said and swiftly crossed the room to reverently slip the photographs into his nightstand drawer. "It's not the right time."

* * *

Abby couldn't help but smile at Brett's wanting to make a good impression. Maybe rinsing the dishes. Picking clothes off the floor. Stashing fishing gear in a closet.

She walked slowly toward the cabin, allowing him extra time as she savored her rustic surroundings. Her Singing Rock memories were fuzzy, sort of like remembering something from a dream. A good dream. She'd forgotten those family times in the spring when few tourists had arrived yet or later in the fall when they'd vacated their summer dwellings. Dad's RV park and campground was like that, too. Fun in the summer with all the newcomers and repeat visitors underfoot, but special in the off-season, too, when the town returned to the locals and wasn't all about catering to out-of-towners.

Today was reminiscent of those lighthearted days, and she was so thankful she'd had the opportunity to apologize and explain herself to Brett. She hadn't wanted to make excuses for how she'd reacted, but felt he needed to know the why behind it. Things felt better between them now.

"You sure are poky." Hat pushed back on his head and arms folded, Brett leaned against the open door's framework. "Get yourself on in here, ma'am."

She couldn't help but notice how the rolled-up sleeves of his shirt revealed well-muscled arms and how the corners of his eyes crinkled in amusement. He was one good-lookin' cowboy, that was for certain. Kindhearted. Fun, too. The latter was a word she'd never have associated with her former fiancé. Speaking of whom, she hadn't heard from him today. Had he finally given up?

Taking her own sweet time, she stepped up onto the porch and playfully sashayed past him and into the dimness of the cabin. It took a few moments for her eyes to adjust from the bright June sunshine, but once they did she realized the interior was every bit as dear on the inside as it was on the outside.

A nightstand and double bed with a Navajo-patterned blanket snuggled in the far corner, a kitchenette with a small table filled a space to the right of the door. The natural stone fireplace was flanked by a sofa, easy chair and end tables and a wide-screen TV was the final trapping signaling this was a man cave for sure. But in her mind's eye she could envision the plaid curtains at the window replaced by lacy ones and the bed covered in a patterned quilt with ruffled throw pillows.

She quickly glanced at Brett, who'd followed her inside and was now watching her assess his home. What was she doing mentally redecorating his quarters?

"I'm almost certain this is the same cabin we played in as kids," she said matter-of-factly, as if that's what had been going through her mind. "I remember the kitchen with the window over the sink. I washed plenty of doll dishes there. And I remember the mullioned windows on either side of the fireplace, too, and the—"

She stopped to stare at the mantel. "Oh, my goodness, these must be your nieces and nephews."

"That they are."

Astounded, she crossed the wood-planked floor to the thick shelf jammed with framed photos from one end of its wood-grained surface to the next. Smiling faces of toddlers to older teens gazed back at her. "You weren't kidding, were you? You practically have your own village here."

Smiling, he came to stand by her. "More than my fair share I'd say, ranging from age four to a freshman in college."

She searched the photographed faces, trying to pick out any resemblance to Uncle Brett.

"How do you keep them all straight?"

"Except for Geri's twins—the two redheads there on the swings—they've all come one at a time, so I've been able to get them fixed in my mind before the next one comes along. But I admit it's hard when I don't often get back to the ranch when everyone is there together. I blink and suddenly a bald-headed baby in diapers is driving."

She pointed to a little girl. "This one looks like she might take after you. She has that same glint in her eyes."

He leaned in to study the photo of the sandy-haired toddler. "I have a glint?"

"You always look like you know a secret the rest of the world hasn't been let in on yet."

"You think so?" He turned to her, that infamous glint sparking. Her heartbeat stepped up the pace.

"I once saw a plaque in a gift shop window that reminds me of you. It said 'When Irish eyes are smiling, they're usually up to something.' Are you Irish?"

He shrugged and glanced away. "Could be, I suppose."

Apparently genealogy wasn't one of his interests. She studied the photos again, marveling that he came from such a huge family. A close one, he'd said. A pang of envy pricked her heart. "I guess we should find those refinishing supplies. I need to get back to the house before Joe leaves for work at two, and I've already used up more than your lunch hour."

"I'll be working this evening, so it will be made up."

Outside once again, Brett took her around the side of the cabin to a shed, where, with brief instructions she'd probably never remember, he gathered up paint dissolvent and needed tools and placed them in a bucket, which he handed to her.

As they arrived back at the truck, a high-pitched childish voice cried out, "Bwett! Bwett!"

From the Singing Rock lodge a little girl with shoulder-length, dark brown curls launched herself off the front steps and came running as fast as her tiny tennis-shoe-clad feet could bring her.

A laughing Olivia followed slowly behind as three-year-old Angie raced, arms outstretched, right into Brett's welcoming ones.

Abby had met the child on one of her first evenings back in Canyon Springs, an awkward meeting, with the toddler insistently reaching out to Abby to be held. Fortunately, the child had eyes solely for Brett at the moment.

"Hey, pumpkin!" He swept her high into the air and she squealed with delight, yet another child who'd been captured by the cowboy's charms.

They chatted with Olivia for a few minutes, Abby noticing the curious light in her cousin's eyes when she looked from Brett to Abby and back again. Then, when Brett said he had to take Abby home and get back to Duffy's, Angie's mother pried the wailing toddler from his arms.

As they left Singing Rock behind, Brett shook his head. "I sure hate leaving them howling like that."

"Isn't that every man's dream?" she couldn't help but tease. "A swooning female throwing herself into your arms? It seems to be the norm around Canyon Springs from what I've heard."

He cut her an impish look. "Is that what you're thinking of doing, too?"

She drew back. "What?"

"Well," he said, his gaze lingering on her, "you seem to know what all these women are doing when it comes to me, so I'm wondering if you're so inclined, as well."

Her face warmed as she drew herself up, chin lifting. "I mention it because—" Because why? Because it was fun to flirt with Brett Marden? But now look at the corner she'd backed herself into.

"I'm all ears."

He might be all ears, but she had to be all red-faced. "Because—"

As they paused at the entrance to the highway, he leaned over and gently cupped her knee with his hand, his eyes alight with mischief. "Take it easy, Abby, I'm just giving you a hard time."

She cast him an exasperated look. "No fooling."

With a chuckle, he put his hand back on the steering wheel. "As far as the ladies go, I'll remind you not to believe anything you hear and only half of what you see. If I find myself saddled with a reputation of sorts, it's because I'm a single man who enjoys the company of women. Just as I do with my sisters, I like making them smile and feel good about themselves. I won't apologize for that."

Why was he making sure she got that sisterly thing straight? Because he wanted it to be clear that when he paid her any attention she wasn't to read anything more into it? Or because he wanted her to know the attention he gave the *others* held no deeper meaning?

"I wasn't asking for an apology. I was pointing out that you have more than a few fans."

He cut her an amused look. "Admit it, Abby."

A butterfly did a three-sixty in her stomach. She narrowed her eyes. "Admit what?"

"You like me."

She shook her head, barely able to suppress a smile. "You have an ego that won't quit."

He laughed. "Tell me something I *don't* know."

The brightness of the day suddenly faded.

If she could garner the courage, she *could* tell him that despite enjoying his company, appreciating his listening ear and loving his laugh, she couldn't allow herself to hope for anything more than a friendship. For if any man deserved to be a dad, it was Brett Marden.

Chapter Thirteen

"What are you doing here so early?"

Brett's spirits lifted as Abby joined him at the back of the garage, where he'd been painting brush-and-roller-style. With the breezy weather, he'd given up on the plan to rent a professional-grade sprayer.

"I don't seem to be catching a break to paint after work what with the red flag warnings. That wind's supposed to gust into the forty-mile-per-hour range by midmorning. And your dad's right—that pine pollen is going to break loose any day now. So I'm trying for plan B, getting here at the crack of dawn while it's still calm."

Gazing at a smiling Abby, her hair falling freely around her shoulders, memories of their time together the previous day swam to the surface. He enjoyed talking to her. Teasing her. She was more than easy to be around. Low maintenance, which wasn't the impression he'd had of her that first day they'd met. The sadness that surrounded her seemed to have lifted somewhat, too, and he couldn't help but hope he'd played a part in that.

But he was still guilt-ridden about hiding Jeremy's photos. Why had he done that? She likely wouldn't have noticed another little boy in that sea of faces.

And what if she had?

What was he so afraid of?

That's the question his sister pinned him with last night when she urged him to open up to Abby about Melynda. She said he had nothing to be ashamed of because of the divorce, that he'd done everything possible to hold things together. He figured Geri thought disclosing that would be a step in the direction of telling her about Jeremy, too, but he wasn't in any hurry to go there. Besides, he might not have anything to be ashamed of, but he wasn't proud of having failed to be the kind of husband a woman would want to keep around. That wasn't a shortcoming he cared to announce to the world, let alone to a woman whose company he was coming to enjoy.

Abby looked up at the barely moving pine limbs overhead. "At least it's nice out here now. It's only sixty-four degrees, but already eighty in Tucson. I think I could get used to summers up here."

"You have a whole one stretching out in front of you, if you're so inclined."

"I can't say it's not tempting, but Tucson's home."

"It doesn't have to be, does it?" He shot her a probing look. "Janet Logan told me a few weeks ago that she's put in for retirement, so there will be a librarian position posted any day now."

"It's still a split between the high school and elementary-middle school?" Was that interest he heard in her voice?

"Right. You should give it serious thought. If you lived here, you could get to know your dad gradually, more naturally. It would take the pressure off that I sense you're both feeling right now. Building relationships isn't an open-the-packet-and-just-add-water deal."

Now why'd he say that? Sure, he enjoyed Abby's company, but it was doubtful living in a town of fewer than three thousand souls had been her lifelong dream. Even if she and her dad worked things out between them, it would

be a stretch for her to settle down here. It could be a repeat performance of her mother's experience just waiting
to happen.

Her pretty mouth dipped into a frown. "Unfortunately,
I doubt I have the experience the school district needs following on the heels of Mrs. Logan. I had that hammered
home late yesterday when I got a call that I wasn't selected
for the second round of interviews for a position I'd applied for in the Tucson area."

"That doesn't mean you wouldn't qualify here." He
squatted to roll the cylinder in the paint trough, then stood
and carefully applied it to the garage wall's surface. "I once
heard Meg say small towns can be a good place to get your
foot in the door. They have limited budgets and often can't
afford the more experienced folks. Janet mentioned that
the current library assistants either don't have the educa-
tional background or an interest in taking on the full load."

She gave a wistful sigh. "I have to admit, I wouldn't
mind living closer to Davy. We've had fun this week and
he's helping me refinish the rocker. That brush-on paint
remover worked like a charm, so I put the rocker in the
garage for safekeeping last night. Did you see it when you
got your supplies out this morning?"

"I did. The two of you did a great job, so you're ready
for the sanding phase. I'll borrow back that paint remover
and get started on the table when I get home tonight." He
glanced toward the house. "So is Davy up yet?"

"Ohhhh, yes. You haven't heard him? I imagine it won't
be long and the whole yard will be filled with neighborhood children. When I talked to Meg last night, she said
they congregated here last summer, which is fine with her
so she can keep an eye on them. But not so lucky for child-
challenged me." Abby laughed. "I may have to call on you
for some little red schoolhouse backup."

"You'll do fine. But I have noticed kids seem to get

outside to play quite a bit in Canyon Springs. More so than when I lived in Phoenix. Even in the cooler winter months it was relatively rare to see many of them outside after school and on weekends. They were indoors, glued to the TV or computer monitor or texting their friends."

Abby tilted her head. "You lived in Phoenix? That surprises me. I'd have thought growing up on a ranch that you'd have been content to stay there and fulfill every little boy's dream."

Cowboying had been Jeremy's dream. He'd wanted to be one like his daddy and grandpa and great-grandpa. It had been heart-wrenching to give his pony away, even to his cousins.

"I have to admit that concrete, skyscrapers and Valley of the Sun heat aren't a combination that call my name. But I did live and work there for five years after..." Catching himself, he let his sentence drift off and abruptly turned to scroll the roller along the side of the garage.

"After what?"

A muscle tightened in his stomach. Here was the opening he'd insisted to Geri that he hadn't been given. She stubbornly said she'd pray for one. Why'd her prayers get faster responses than his? He didn't want to expose his failings to a woman whose admiration he'd only started to realize he longed to attain.

"After what?" she said again, giving him a playful smile that under any other circumstances would have set off fireworks inside him. "After you saved the world from aliens?"

"Nothing so heroic, unfortunately." Reluctantly, he set the roller aside and turned to meet Abby's inquisitive gaze. Swallowed hard. "I lived in Phoenix after... I'm divorced, Abby."

He heard a soft intake of breath as her smile faded. There was no mistaking the confusion—and disappointment—in her eyes. That little disclosure sure put a damper on the day.

"It's not something I share with many," he continued, filling the awkward silence. "But I should probably have told you sooner."

Her solemn gaze held his. "I'm…sorry."

Sorry because he'd gone through the trauma of a divorce? Or sorry because he'd lost some luster in her eyes?

"My wife left me seven years ago." Jeremy dying in his arms—not Melynda's—had been the last straw. She'd never forgiven him—or God—for that. "It wasn't a happy time in my life."

"I don't imagine it was," she said softly, now avoiding his gaze. Was she wondering why he hadn't mentioned this yesterday when she'd told him about her mother abandoning her dad? Could she understand now why he told her she should tell Bill she didn't think the breakup with her mother was all his fault?

The silence between them stretched uncomfortably. Should he offer her more explanation? Confess he'd failed to be the husband his wife needed him to be? That the practice of his fledgling faith had driven her away?

"You always wonder," he said, his tone flat, emotionless, "what you could have done differently to prevent things from coming to that point. I thought I'd done everything possible, all the right things. But it still fell apart. Melynda could never understand, considering the things life had dealt us, how I could put my faith in God."

"You weren't believers when you married?"

"No. We were both good, decent folks but, despite our upbringing, not actively interested in the things of God."

"So, what—"

"Aunt Abby! Aunt Abby!"

They turned to see Davy dash down the back porch steps and race toward them, arms flailing and his smile wide. "Daddy just called! He said to tell you Mom's having a baby!"

*   *   *

The hospital's sharp, familiar odor curled through Abby's memory Saturday afternoon. She choked back a wave of nausea as she, Dad, Sharon and Davy traversed the hospital's labyrinth of hallways in search of baby Jori. She hadn't expected the sounds, scents and sights of the regional medical center to so violently intrude on what should have been a happy trek to see a newborn who'd put in an appearance at sunrise that morning.

Davy gave a little skip as he tugged at her hand. "Are we almost there, Aunt Abby?"

"Almost."

She hadn't wanted to come, preferring to linger behind and pack her belongings so she'd be ready to depart the minute Meg returned home. But Dad insisted. What excuse could she provide without making it appear she didn't want to go because Sharon was accompanying them?

But the antiseptic odor now pressed in close. Too close. Medical personnel passed by, speaking in urgent whispers. The intercom's crackle and the squeak of shoes on the tiles further heightened the tension seizing her limbs.

She tightened her grip on Davy's hand, drawing reassurance from its warmth. He looked up at her curiously and she forced a smile, focusing on putting one foot in front of the other. After all, she was there to see her brother's baby, not to have her inner organs scrutinized and to be told yet again that they were lacking—that *she* was lacking—and nothing could be done about it.

Last winter, while on her month-long holiday break, she'd spent endless hours in the waiting and examination rooms of an area hospital. There'd been hours spent praying that the initial diagnosis from her premarital exam with a new physician had been incorrect. After all, her now-retired former doctor hadn't mentioned any possible inability to bear children in all the years she'd gone to him.

When the invasive exams had confirmed suspicions, her fiancé had again insisted on further testing. He'd flown with her to Los Angeles for another battery of distressing tests—and informed her on the flight home that given the circumstances...

She squeezed Davy's hand again as another set of automatic doors opened before them. How could she ever have thought she wanted to be married to a man like Gene Daymert? The man couldn't even wait to get to a private location before he poured out his displeasure in her physiological shortcomings, acting almost as if she'd led him on, deceived him, promised something she couldn't deliver—his baby.

She took a ragged breath, trying to tune out her sterile surroundings. It was human nature to doubt God's goodness when bad things happened, so she needed to remind herself of the many good gifts she'd been given. She'd done her best for months to do that. But for some reason, coming to Canyon Springs stirred it up all over again.

"You okay, doll?" Sharon whispered as Davy relinquished her hand and he and his grandpa moved rapidly toward a bank of interior windows that revealed a row of tiny baby beds. "You look pale."

"Oh, I'm fine." But she hung back, glancing around the corridor. "I'm wondering which room is Meg's."

"You don't want to see the baby?"

"I'd like to visit with Meg first." She needed to sit down. Maybe drink a glass of water.

"If I'm not mistaken, that's Joe coming now. He just left the room with the balloons around the door." Sharon patted her arm, then turned to join Davy and his grandpa.

"Hey, sis." Joe gave Abby a big hug. "Have you seen what a beautiful baby your big brother produced?"

"You're a modest one. I think Meg deserves some credit, don't you?"

"Mmm, maybe a little." He pinched his thumb and forefinger together, then laughed. "Come over here and take a look."

"You go and have family time with Davy. I'd like to see Meg for a few minutes, if she's taking visitors. The balloon room?"

"Right. But hurry back. I'll see if they'll let you hold her."

That was exactly what she *didn't* want. Taking a deep breath, she walked briskly to her sister-in-law's open door and knocked. "Anybody home?"

"Abby!" In the dimly lit room, Meg waved from the hospital bed, where she rested against its raised back. She looked tired, but there was a happy glow nevertheless. "Come join us."

Us?

Abby stepped through the door, her eyes adjusting to the subdued lighting. The Canyon Springs grapevine must have been sizzling with the birth announcement that morning for there, in the chair she'd hoped to sink into next to Meg's bed, sat Brett. He looked at her sharply, then stood and motioned for her to take his seat.

She must look even worse than she felt, but she remained standing.

"I was in town to drop off a piece of equipment for repair and decided to check out the new addition to the Diaz household."

"He brought me those." As Brett moved to join Abby at the door, Meg pointed at a bouquet of assorted flowers, their subtle scent perfuming the air and thankfully neutralizing the antiseptic smell. "Aren't they beautiful?"

Brett gave Abby a nod, his eyes twinkling. "That Jori's a beauty, too, isn't she?"

"I...haven't seen her yet."

"You drove all the way over here and you haven't seen

her?" He cocked an eyebrow, then playfully reached out to snag her arm, intending to twirl her around and head her back toward the door.

She balked. "We just got here and I want Davy and his dad to have one-on-one time with her. I thought I could catch a few minutes with Meg."

"Got it. Girl time." He took a step back, but his gaze lingered on her. "I'll take the hint and bid you ladies adieu."

Once he left, Abby rounded the bed to pull a Dixie cup from a dispenser by the sink and fill it. Then she eased herself into the vacated chair and took a sip. No one would guess from Brett's chipper countenance that he'd shared with her a darker side of his life yesterday. He'd implied his wife had left him because of his faith, but there had to be more to it.

She managed a smile in Meg's direction. "Davy's so excited about Jori that I could hardly get him to eat his lunch so we could bring him over here."

"Things have gone well this past week?"

"I was concerned when Joe asked me to stay and watch him, but Davy's made it easy. Has he had any complaints about me?"

"None. Some people are gifted in the mothering department and you're one of them."

Abby glanced away. She didn't want to talk about mothering.

"Joe said you were turned down on that Tucson job. I know that's disappointing, but maybe it's a God thing and you're supposed to apply for Janet Logan's position instead. What would it hurt? Throw your hat in the ring and, if God wants you here, you'll get it."

"But what if I don't *want* to apply for it, Meg?"

"Why not? I love Canyon Springs myself, and I grew up in a big town like you did. What if nothing opens up elsewhere and you change your mind after the position here has been filled? You can always make up your mind when it's offered, right?" Mischief suddenly lit Meg's eyes. "Besides, I get the impression that Brett Marden would like you to stick around."

Then it was good she'd be leaving soon.

"In case you haven't figured it out, he turns on the charm around all women. He even admits it's all in fun. Nothing serious. He claims he thinks of women as if they are his sisters."

"I guarantee you he never looked at his sisters the way he was looking at you today." Meg gave a happy sigh. "He's going to make some lucky woman a wonderful husband. Why not you?"

"He's not my type."

"Let's see... Good-looking guy. Serious about God. Kind, fun, dad material." Meg ticked off each plus on her fingers. "Yeah, I can see how that might turn you off."

Abby made a face. "Very funny."

"Come on, think what cute babies the two of you could make."

A knot jerked in Abby's stomach. There would be no babies.

Before she could respond, Joe stepped into the room and headed directly to the bed to bestow a kiss on Meg's waiting lips. "Who would make cute babies with my little sister?"

"Brett."

"Really?" He looked over at Abby, his eyes alight with curiosity. "I thought you said you weren't interested in a cowboy."

"I'm not." She rose from her chair to move to the door, once again feeling closed in. Trapped.

Meg's eyes appealed with sudden concern. "We were just teasing, Abby. Having fun."

Joe and Meg meant no harm, but even though she told

herself to "just get over it," the hospital atmosphere and baby talk were too much for her. She paused in the doorway, then forced a lightness into her tone. "You can have all the fun you want when Meg's mom arrives and I leave town. Which will be tomorrow."

With a breezy wave, she turned away, eager to escape.

"Wait, Abby!" Her brother's voice riveted her to the ground. "Didn't Dad tell you? Meg's mom can't come after all."

Chapter Fourteen

"Do I get to see the kiddo today?" Hat in hand, Brett stood at the back door right after lunchtime Tuesday afternoon.

He looked especially handsome today, so genuinely eager to see her new niece again. Abby sighed inwardly. She'd have been back in Tucson by now, if Meg's mother hadn't sprained an ankle. When Joe made that unwelcome announcement Saturday, she hadn't even flinched. Not much anyway. It seemed circumstances were conspiring to keep her in Canyon Springs.

Nevertheless, she'd slipped in and out the back way at church on Sunday in order to avoid Brett. Then on Brett's Monday off, when he came to work on the garage and take Davy boot shopping, she insisted she had to help Meg and the baby settle in.

"Jori's sleeping," Abby informed him, hoping he'd decide to come back later. Like when Meg's mother finally made it up from the Valley.

"Never mind that," Meg called softly from the kitchen table. "Get yourself in here, Brett."

As he entered and popped his hat atop the refrigerator, Meg rose slowly to her feet, beckoning for him to follow her into the living room. Abby trailed behind as Brett joined her sister-in-law at the beribboned wicker bassinet.

He made a cradling motion with his arms. "May I?"

Meg nodded and he expertly lifted the infant into his arms. Jori didn't wake, but snuggled contentedly toward his chest. Abby's heart beat a dirge at the sight of her niece cradled there. She looked so tiny, safe and secure. So right. And Brett's face? Alive with joy as he gazed down at the little bundle.

"You're better at this than I am," Meg said, her tone admiring. "You handle her like a pro."

"You'll be one before you know it, it just takes practice." He glanced at Abby, his gaze warm. "As Abby may have already told you, my brothers and sisters have fifteen kids between them so I've had a little more practice than most."

"Fifteen?" Meg's eyes widened. "In that case, let me know if you're hiring out for the night shift."

"She's keeping you awake?"

"All night, every night."

He smiled down at Jori, his voice soft. "You've got your days and nights mixed up, do you, little lady?"

One dark eye peeped open to study him and he gave a pretend gasp. "There you are. Now I'll be in trouble for waking you up."

"Maybe that's what Meg wanted you to do." Abby stepped closer to look into the tiny face. "To wake her up and keep her awake so she'll sleep better tonight."

Brett shifted Jori in his arms, then looked to Abby. "Do you want to hold her?"

"No." She quickly stepped back. "I mean, I think she's quite content where she is at the moment."

Brett's querying gaze briefly held hers before again focusing on the child. Jori's eyes drifted closed and he gently placed her back in the bassinet. "Sorry, Meg, looks like she's down for the count again."

"Oh, well, nice try."

He looked again at Abby, "I have to get back to Duffy's, but do you have a minute?"

"Sure." What else could she say? Reluctantly she followed him onto the back porch, not looking forward to hearing him gush over the preciousness of her new niece. *Get a grip, Abby.*

He turned to her as he settled his hat on his head. "Would you like to join me in experiencing a genuine taste of small-town life? There's an ice cream social at the church Friday night. More than ice cream actually. Sandwiches, too."

"Thanks, but—"

He held up a halting hand, the twinkle in his eyes dimming. "You're seeing someone special down in Tucson, aren't you?"

Where'd he get that idea? He'd taken a risk telling her about his ex-wife, yet she'd kept silent about her own relational failures. She didn't want to tell him about the reason for the breakup, but what would it hurt to let him know she had been involved with someone, too?

"I'm not seeing anyone at the moment. But five months ago I broke up with my fiancé. The engagement didn't last long. Maybe five weeks. Irreconcilable differences."

There, she got that over with.

Brett appeared to give her words some thought. "I'm sorry to hear that."

"It was for the best."

He stepped off the porch, then turned to her again, abruptly changing the subject. "Are you bringing Davy to riding lessons this afternoon?"

"No. His friend Gina's mother will be taking both of them."

He scuffed a booted toe in the dirt. "Okay. Well, then,

give me a call if you change your mind about the ice cream social. Joe has my number."

"I will." But she wouldn't. No good could come of spending more time together.

When Brett departed, Abby joined Meg at the kitchen table for a glass of lemonade.

Her sister-in-law gave a wistful sigh. "I don't think Brett came here to see Jori as much as he did to see you. He certainly looked at you more than he did her."

"I hadn't noticed." She'd been too into her own thoughts, watching him with her niece.

"I'm not trying to make you uncomfortable, Abby, but he shows all the signs of being interested in you."

She was interested in him, too, yet that didn't change her circumstances. But she may as well let Meg partially know where things stood. "A few minutes ago he invited me to the church ice cream social."

Meg sat up straighter, eyes brightening. "So you have a date?"

"I turned him down."

"You're kidding. Why?" Meg stared at Abby as if she were a hopeless case. "This guy's not only going to make some lucky woman a fabulous husband, but he'll be a good dad to their kids, too. Did you see how comfortable he was around Jori? He's already kid-broke. Can't ask for better than that."

"Did you know he's divorced?" Brett said he'd told very few people, but surely her sister-in-law knew.

Meg raised a skeptical brow. "Who told you that?"

"He did."

She sat back in her chair. "Wow. That blows me away. I've known him for over a year and I had no idea."

"It shocked me, too."

"Did they have kids? Did he say what happened to break them up?"

"He didn't mention children, but I think he would have, don't you?"

"As crazy as he is about them," Meg confirmed, "he would have."

"We were interrupted and haven't had the opportunity to talk about any of this since then." Maybe that's why he wanted her to go to the church event? "But apparently she left him. Something to do with his growing faith. Differing beliefs."

"I hadn't heard even a whisper of anything like that." Meg motioned helplessly. "I can't imagine any woman in her right mind leaving a guy like Brett."

"She must have had her reasons." Abby reached for her glass and took a sip. "We don't have all the facts, so it wouldn't be right to blame his ex for everything. It takes two to tango."

"I agree, but if she left him because of his faith…"

Obviously, Meg thought the guy could do no wrong. "People see things from their own point of view, put their own spin on things to place themselves in the best light. We all do it. I can hardly think Brett is any different."

How did she get off on this tangent? While it might divert Meg from grilling her on her reasons for steering clear of him, her real reason for avoiding Brett had nothing to do with his past. It had to do with *her* present.

"No, but still…" Meg studied her for a long moment. "This is about your ex-fiancé, isn't it?"

Abby stiffened.

"You showed him the door," Meg continued, "so you're taking Brett's ex's side to validate your own choices, to justify your calling it quits."

"Believe me, it's not the same."

"Maybe not, but don't allow what happened to you to negatively color Brett's history. I think he told you about this because he trusts you to weigh it carefully. Fairly. He took quite a risk in sharing that part of his life, which tells me he's coming to care for you."

Abby stood and moved to the refrigerator to put away the lemonade pitcher. Did she dare tell Meg about her inability to have a child? Would she then understand the impossibility of the situation? No, she couldn't tell her now, not with Jori sleeping in the next room and Meg happier than she'd ever been in her whole life with husband, home, son and daughter.

She leaned against the counter. "My ex-fiancé has been calling me almost daily since I came here."

"Oh." Disappointment flickered through Meg's eyes. "Then you two are getting back together, I guess."

"No. In fact, I haven't taken any of his calls."

"Why not?"

"Because…" She was treading on dangerous ground here if Meg insisted on more details than she was willing to share. "I didn't dump him as I've let all of you assume. He dumped me. Nevertheless, I now realize we weren't a good fit. At all. Just like Brett and I wouldn't be a fit."

Meg gave an exasperated snort. "Joe and I almost missed the boat because we had misconceptions about each other. Fears that had us by the throat. There's no such thing as a perfect relationship, but you follow God's lead, make a commitment and stick to it. You grow and mature and love each other for a lifetime."

"I'm not falling in love with Brett and he's not falling in love with me." That would be too much to hope for, that a man like Brett, who was crazy about kids, would love her enough to overlook things Gene had been unwilling to.

"Are you sure about that, Abby? I met your brother in late September and I sounded just like you do. Total denial. But by Thanksgiving we were engaged and married by spring break. My brother met your cousin right before

Labor Day last year and they were engaged by October. Married in December."

"That is not going to happen."

"You never know," Meg persisted in a singsong voice, a knowing gaze pinned on Abby.

"I know."

"She broke up with a fiancé not long ago, Geri." That explained a lot about her skittishness around him and even the underlying sadness. She spoke of the breakup with a casual offhandedness, but he suspected it had been a disappointing chapter in her life.

Brett gazed across the echoing, well-lit arena from where he sat in the upper bleachers taking a break on his Tuesday evening shift. Half a dozen teens and their mounts practiced barrel racing down below, the sound of pounding hooves and the creek of leather reaching his ears.

"So the coast is clear," his sister concluded. "What are you going to do about it? You know you're falling for her."

It wouldn't do any good to deny it. Geri would see right through him.

"Even if circumstances were such that I was free to pursue her, which they aren't, I wouldn't want to barge in and repeat the other guy's mistakes. But her explanation of irreconcilable differences doesn't give me much to go on." Was that vagueness on her part deliberate? "I don't know if she broke up with him or if he broke up with her or if it was by mutual decision."

"Does it matter?"

"Maybe. Her mom ran out on her dad when Abby was little."

"So you think she's genetically wired to dump men who come into her life? You've concluded she sent that guy packing for no better reason than because he parts his hair on the wrong side or uses the wrong brand of toothpaste?"

He stood and started down the bleacher steps. His suspicions that there might be more to Abby's story sounded silly when spelled out like that. Leave it to his sister to make him feel like an idiot.

"I get the impression, little brother, that you're assessing your so-called friendship with a futuristic bent."

Yeah, he guessed he *was* evaluating her ability to commit to a lasting relationship. He'd already been abandoned by one woman and he sure didn't want to get hit over the head with a repeat performance.

"As you pointed out," Geri continued, "you're only getting to know each other. But you've never cared for women who blurt out every thought that enters their head, so I'd say that's a point in her favor not to have elaborated on the circumstances of her broken engagement. And personally—"

Did he really want to hear it?

"—I think you're throwing up red flags. You're trying to find something wrong with Abby so you can justify slinking off into the shadows again and not having to deal with the CF issue."

"There's nothing wrong with being cautious."

"Melynda abandoned you because she couldn't handle the tough times. She resented your turning to God. She remarried and moved on with her life. What's wrong with you moving on, too?"

He halted on the steps, his gaze once again roaming the vastness of the arena as the throaty whinny of a horse carried from the stable. "If you have all the answers, then tell me this. Why didn't God get hold of her like He did me when Jeremy was diagnosed with CF? Why didn't my turning to Him, changing my life, lead her to Him, as well?"

That guilt had eaten at him for seven years. Didn't the

Bible talk about how the way a believing spouse lived could win the partner, too?

"Two words, Brett," Geri said softly. "Free will. You made a choice to turn to God and she made a choice not to. She made a choice to leave the marriage. You didn't."

He tightened his grip on the phone. "Regardless, I think it's clear I'm not ready to be involved with Abby, with any woman, right now."

"The fact that Abby told you she'd been engaged sounds as if it's something she wanted you to know. Have you told her about Melynda?"

"I did."

"And how did she take that?"

He released a pent-up breath. "She didn't say a whole lot, but then we haven't had the opportunity to discuss it after being interrupted on Friday. I feel, though, that she stepped back. Withdrew."

He'd tested the waters today by asking her to the ice cream social. And got a flat turndown. That made things pretty clear.

"It could be she needs time to think things over. To pray about it. From what you've told me, it's not like your marriage is common knowledge. It probably caught her off guard."

"Maybe." And maybe it *was* time to sit down with Abby and clear the air. His sister was right. He could let this promising friendship slip through his fingers or he could step up to the plate and face the things he'd been avoiding.

This limbo world of indecisiveness had gone on long enough. He'd always been one to take the bull by the horns, but this waffling pattern he'd fallen into since Abby came on the scene was unacceptable. He needed to discuss with her his marriage to Melynda and be open to honestly answering questions she might have. He needed to ask her about her engagement. What worked? What hadn't worked? And he had to be willing to tell her about Jeremy—and the medical issues surrounding getting involved with Jeremy's dad.

And then if she said she wasn't interested, so be it.

He squared his shoulders. If God would provide the opportunity, he'd speak up.

"What would you say, Geri, if I told you I've come to a decision?"

Chapter Fifteen

Abby glanced down at the caller ID midmorning Wednesday and tensed. "It's Gene again. I thought he'd given up."

Meg lifted a concerned gaze from where she rinsed salad greens at the sink. "You're going to have to talk to him eventually, aren't you, Abby? Why not now?"

She didn't know why he kept calling and she still wasn't sure she wanted to know. But she was stronger now than she'd been five months ago. Perhaps more, even, than she'd been a few weeks ago. She didn't know if Brett had found a physician for the kids' camp, but this could be the opportunity to ask Gene to put in a good word with his sister, to keep the conversation on a less personal level if that was his intent.

Please, God, make this as painless as possible. Abby stepped into the living room. "Hello, Gene."

"Where have you been?" *No hello, Abby. Good to hear your voice. It's been a while.* "Your mom said you're out of town and her housekeeper won't even speak to me."

How like Gene that sounded. Her mother had pegged him as impatient. Why hadn't she noticed that before? It wasn't that he was a bad man by any means, despite his uncompassionate dismissal of her. He had a personal life plan fixed in his mind, much like the class syllabus he faithfully followed each semester and didn't appreciate departures from.

Like the one she'd thrown at him last winter.

"I'm still out of town. What's up?"

He cleared his throat. "I guess I want to apologize."

She hadn't expected that. Not really, even though she'd envisioned such a scenario in her mind for months after their breakup.

"For?"

"For the way I broke off our engagement."

She stepped to a window and gazed out at the pines, praying God would give her the words she needed.

"It was for the best." Isn't that what she'd told Brett?

"No, no, I'm not so sure of that now."

Abby's stomach lurched.

"I've had time to think about it," he continued, his voice further softening, "and I think we should reconsider."

She closed her eyes momentarily. Months ago she'd dreamed of hearing those words, but now they didn't sound so sweet.

"Abby? I said I think we should reconsider. Sit down and talk things over. Reevaluate."

"Nothing has changed." Except that her eyes had been opened to the fact that this man wasn't for her. "I couldn't have children last winter and I can't have children in June."

She glanced through the doorway into the kitchen. Meg's hands, poised over the sink, had suddenly stilled.

"Not so fast," Gene cautioned.

This man who'd all but knocked her down trying to get out the door of their engagement was telling *her* not so fast?

"We had a good thing going for a while," he persisted. "A comfortable relationship."

Brett's teasing smile flashed through her mind, how he enjoyed pushing her out of her comfort zone. "Sometimes comfortable isn't all it's cracked up to be. When you learned I was incapable of bearing children, it wasn't comfortable for either of us."

"But I just said I've given that additional thought. I recently learned of another professor who shares our same dilemma. He and his wife contracted with a surrogate to—"

"Gene? If your intent is to initiate a dialogue leading to a reengagement, you can save your breath."

She didn't mean to sound so harsh, but there was no point in allowing the conversation to continue along its apparent path. For a long moment Gene was silent and she glanced into the kitchen. Meg, who'd given up pretending she wasn't listening, nodded in silent agreement.

"I've found a resolution to our situation, but I didn't think you'd reject it without due consideration." Gene's placating tone irritated. "However, I'm cognizant of the fact that it took time to get used to the idea myself, so I'm willing to extend that opportunity to you, as well."

"It's not about children anymore. It's about us. Our relationship wasn't a healthy one. Not for me anyway."

"I don't know where this is coming from," he blustered, his ego finally getting the picture that there would be no reengagement. No woman to raise his children given birth by another.

"It's coming from my heart. I'm sorry. Goodbye, Gene."

When she'd shut off the phone, she stood silent for several long minutes. She hadn't wanted their conversation to end on such a negative note. She hadn't intended to be rude, just clear. This was a man she'd cared for, one she'd considered marrying. And yet…

Brett once again drifted into her thoughts. He and Gene were nothing alike, yet both wanted children she couldn't give them. Gene might not have the makings of a good parent, but Brett did. Children loved him and he loved them. He even devoted his free time to kid-related events like… A soft whimper escaped her lips. *The kids' camp.*

She'd forgotten to ask Gene about his sister and there was no way she could call him back now.

"Abby? Are you okay?"

Meg had stepped to the living room door, her gaze intent.

She sighed. "Yes. But I let Brett and Janet down. I meant to ask Gene to approach his physician sister about filling in at a local camp for kids with disabilities."

"From the sound of the conversation, I think you had other things on your mind." Meg's eyes filled with tears, her voice filled with compassion. "You can't have babies?"

Abby tightened her lips to keep them from trembling. "No. No little ones for me, I'm afraid."

"Oh, sweetie." Her sister-in-law approached and pulled her into a bear hug. "Why didn't you tell us? Being here for Jori's birth, taking care of Davy… Joe and I'd never have put you through that if we'd have known."

"I know you wouldn't have." Abby returned the hug, then stepped back, thankful that her own tears remained in check. "I didn't want to ruin such a happy time."

"I take it your ex-fiancé wants to get back together, even though the two of you can't have children?"

Abby scoffed halfheartedly. "He has it all figured out. He'll acquire a surrogate to carry his child. All I have to do is step back into his life and change their diapers. Can you believe it?"

She shook her head, the reality of Gene's "offer" still not quite sinking in.

"I understand now, though," Meg said, softly, wiping away her own tears, "your hesitation in getting involved with Brett. I'm sorry I kept teasing you about him."

"I really like him. A lot. But you can see now why it

can't work, can't you? Even you think he was born to be a dad."

"But there *is* a thing called adoption." Meg's still-wobbly smile encouraged, an underlying fierceness in her tone. "I didn't give birth to Davy, but I love him as my own."

"I wouldn't want Brett to make that sacrifice."

"Aren't you making assumptions based on your unfortunate experience with that annoyingly stupid ex-fiancé of yours?"

Was she?

"I can't exactly walk up to Brett and announce something like this so early in our relationship."

"No, but what if you applied for that librarian position, got it and moved to Canyon Springs? What if you and Brett took your time getting to know each other?"

Was that an option? Hope sparked somewhere deep inside.

Abby nibbled at her lower lip. "Brett said something similar in regard to Dad. He said I'm putting too much pressure on myself and Dad by expecting everything to come together overnight."

"Maybe Brett wasn't just planting that seed in your mind as it relates to your father, but to him, too."

"That sounds nice, but I can see so many ways moving here could go wrong on all counts."

"Abby." Meg placed her hands on her hips. "Do you believe God is in control? Do you believe He has a good plan for your life or not?"

Did she? Sometimes her faith seemed so weak, so undernourished, that it wasn't even funny. "Yeah, I guess I do."

"Well, then? What do you have to lose?"

That afternoon Abby stood silently in the open doorway of a spacious, well-appointed tack room at the High Country Equine Center. Breathing in the rich smell of horses, hay and leather, she watched Brett working at the counter, his back to her as he switched out the bit on a bridle.

She'd thought of calling, telling him she'd take him up on his offer to attend the ice cream social on Friday. She could share her news that night. But she'd been unable to wait, wanting him to be the first, after Meg, to know.

She paused a moment longer in the doorway, reveling in Brett's cheery whistle and watching the muscles play across his back under his shirt. Well-worn boots, faded jeans and that ever-present Western straw hat completed the picture of a real-life cowboy.

She was falling for a *cowboy?*

"I did it," she said softly.

At the sound of her voice, Brett spun toward her with a welcoming smile. "What are you doing here?"

She stepped into the tack room, her insides aflutter at the pleased look in his eyes. Her tropical-print sundress was new, an impulsive purchase from a local shop, but apparently it had been a good choice.

"Didn't you hear me? I said I did it."

Placing the bridle on the counter, he walked over to her, a brow cocked and his hands on his slim hips. "Did what?"

"I applied for the librarian position in Canyon Springs."

His eyes widened. "Are you kidding me?"

She laughed and shook her head.

"Boy howdy!"

To her surprise, he secured his hands around her waist and effortlessly lifted her off her feet to where she looked down into his laughing, upturned face. For a long, breathless moment their joyful gazes met, Abby's spirits soaring that he was as happy about her news as she was. But as the seconds ticked by with their gazes locked, she grew more conscious of Brett's warm, secure grip and the subtle, smoldering flicker in his eyes. Heart pounding, she drew in a breath as he slowly lowered her to her feet. But his hands remained firmly on her waist.

"Boy howdy," he said again softly, his gaze riveted on her face. Her eyes. Her mouth.

She self-consciously wet her lips. She should step back. Move away from him. But her feet remained frozen to the ground. "Remember, applying doesn't mean I'll get the job."

"You'll get it." His voice sounded husky. "I'm praying you will."

As if that settled it.

She took a labored breath, then with every ounce of strength she possessed, she stepped back. For a fleeting moment she thought he might not release her, but to her relief he allowed her to slip from the security of his strong hands.

Another step or two put them at a less intimate distance.

"So, what changed your mind, Abby?" He ducked his head to catch her eye. "About applying, I mean."

She cut him a playful look, hoping to further break the supercharged atmosphere between them. "You."

"Me?"

"Well, I mean you saying that I was putting too much pressure on myself and on my family by walking in the door after eighteen years and expecting everything to be perfect."

"That's what did it?"

Was he disappointed? Did he want her to say it had something to do with him on a more personal level? "I felt a huge weight lift when I finally realized I didn't have to make everything work out today, right now, this very minute. My relationship with Dad doesn't have to depend on a solitary do-or-die meeting and then the door closes."

He nodded, his expression now thoughtful. "If you're here in town, you can get to know each other gradually."

Was he thinking she could get to know him, too?

"You were right. I was putting way too many fragile eggs in one basket, thinking healing and resolution had to take place in one small window of time or it would never happen. Like you, Meg suggested I apply for the job and see if the doors open. So I did."

"Will you stay in town and wait for an interview?"

"I'll probably go back to Tucson. Meg's mother will be coming up to stay at Meg and Joe's place soon and it's a little presumptuous to move in with Dad. Meg said I might have to borrow her aunt Julie's RV so I could have a little independence."

"God works in mysterious ways." Brett reached for her hand and again drew her close.

Too close.

His gaze was steady, too. Serious, as if he had something pressing to tell her. Where was the "natural" and "gradual" element in the steps she'd taken to buy her some time? She wasn't ready to deal with the reality of her situation, to spring it on Brett and force him to prematurely make decisions about them as a couple.

"Abby—"

When he tugged again at her hand, his eyes warming, she impulsively pulled away and snatched the hat from his head. Spinning away from him, she dashed out the tack room door and into the wide box-stall-lined corridor.

"Oh, no, you don't. Get back here."

In spite of her head start, a laughing Brett easily caught up with her. Slipping his arm around her waist, he drew her to a halt and swung her back to face him. And before she could stop him, remind him of where they were, he confidently leaned in to touch his lips to hers.

Startled, breathless, Abby nevertheless found her arms slipping around his neck, his hat still in her hand. The hammer of her heart intensified as he drew her closer and the kiss drew out longer. To her amazement, she'd never been kissed liked this before. A kiss that gave, didn't just take. One that tasted not only of emotion expressed, but of reverence conveyed. That spoke of—did she dare hope it?—the beginning of genuine love?

Her dreams suddenly took flight, pushing aside the disappointments, the reservations, the fears... Brett, her husband, father to their adopted children. Waking up every morning in each other's arms. Laughing their way through each day and holding each other through challenging times.

Could this really be happening?

"Woo-hoo!"

"Way to go, Brett!"

"Pretty hot stuff for an old dude!"

Abby's heart jerked at the sound of catcalls and clapping, heat flooding her cheeks. But while Brett cut off the kiss, he kept his hands secured at her waist, not allowing her to step away as they spotted the lineup of teenage males who'd paused while unloading hay from a pickup just inside the stable's rear entrance. She hadn't even noticed them when she'd made her impulsive escape from the tack room.

"Hope you're taking good notes, *boys*," Brett called out cheerfully. He again turned to her, his eyes dancing, and for a horrifying moment she thought he was going to dip her back for another kiss.

"Don't you dare." Her panicked gaze burned a warning into his. What was she thinking to have allowed him to kiss her like that? And in a public place. It was all in fun for him. He was being, well, Brett. A good-time-guy having a good time.

And then it struck her. What if he wasn't just seizing the moment? What if there was more to it? Yes, she'd been warned that Brett wasn't the type to settle down. But what if he'd come to care for her as much as she did him? She hadn't had the chance to tell him about her medical condition before things went too far between them. He deserved so much more than she could give him—a family of his own.

"Come on, Abby," he said softly, "don't tell me you didn't enjoy that as much as I did."

"I…I don't enjoy being an object of entertainment for teenage voyeurs."

Brett shrugged, a smile twitching. "Who knows? Maybe we'll hit the high ratings on YouTube this week."

"What?" She struggled to step away from him, but he held her tight. "One of them was videoing us?"

"No, no, calm down," he soothed with a chuckle. "I'm just teasing."

To her relief, he gave her waist a final squeeze before releasing her, then turned back to the youthful audience still calling encouragement for the show to go on.

"Back to work, children! Trey's not paying you to stand around all day."

Good-natured boos and hisses echoed down the corridor.

Not waiting to hear any more, she whirled away from Brett and headed in the opposite direction from the teens. She wasn't standing around here one more second, either.

Chapter Sixteen

Where was she going now? She still had his hat.

Waving off the teenagers and their "she's getting away!" cries, Brett headed after her.

Was she mad at him for kissing her or just because they'd been caught by the hired help? That had been some kiss all right. It hadn't been one-sided, either. She'd given back as good as she'd gotten. But how had he let himself get so carried away? He hadn't kissed a woman in over seven years, and out of the blue he couldn't keep his hands off Abby. No wonder she'd taken flight.

Striding down the corridor, he could see sunlight hit her as she emerged from the shadowed stable, her sundress a swirl of vibrant color so unlike what he was used to seeing her in. He picked up the pace, suspecting the teenage hands were getting a hoot out of watching him chase after her. No doubt they'd fill Trey in on all of it, right down to the details. If his employer thought holding hands within ninety minutes of meeting Abby was extreme, what would he think of this?

Just as she arrived at her car on the far, shaded side of the parking lot, he caught up with her. He gently grasped her arm to turn her toward him, but to his shock, an invisible fist socked him in the gut.

She had tears in her eyes.

His heart crumpled. "Hey, what's all this?"

She shook her head, avoiding his gaze.

"They were just having fun, Abby. There was no harm intended."

Her trembling lips tightened. "I know that."

She wasn't upset about the boys? Then it must be him. He hadn't kissed very many women in his life, but this would be the first kiss he'd have to apologize for and he wasn't even sure why.

"I'm sorry. I didn't think a kiss would upset you like this. I thought…that it wasn't unwelcome."

"It's not that…" Her voice broke as she thrust his hat at him and he placed it on the roof of her car.

"I have to be honest, Abby. I don't know when I've ever been quite so confused about a gal, so I know it's my fault for giving you mixed signals. I guess it just struck me today, you know with you saying you might be staying in Canyon Springs, that there might be a chance that we—"

"There isn't."

That stung. But he soldiered on. There were things that needed saying. "I know I got a little ahead of myself and I apologize for that. But what's wrong with two people coming to care for each other? I don't think I'm mistaken that you've taken more than a passing interest in me."

Geri was right. They could work things out, even the CF thing, if they could talk about it openly. Be honest. Make decisions together.

She swiped away a tear. "I apologize if I've given you that impression. It would never work, Brett."

"And why's that?" He ducked his head down, trying to coax a smile. "You don't like cowboy boots? Or I don't shave often enough. Is that it?"

He lifted her hand to gently brush it along his jaw.

She pulled back. "Please stop trying to make me laugh, okay? There are things that you don't know about me that make it unwise to—"

He reached out to playfully caress her soft jawline. "Are you trying to tell me you shave, too?"

She jerked away. "Brett!"

At the desperation in her voice, he finally "got it." Why'd he always try to lighten a serious situation with inappropriate humor? Yet another flaw God needed to get busy working on. "I'm sorry, Abby. Go ahead. You think there are things I don't know about you that make involvement an unwise move."

"It's not that I don't like you, Brett." She momentarily pressed her lips firmly together. "It's just that there's something standing between us that makes a relationship impossible."

"I don't get a say in it? Get to vote on whether or not it's a deal breaker?"

"Believe me, it's a deal breaker." She blinked back tears.

He awkwardly patted her arm. "Hey, now, easy there. Easy there."

Great, Marden, that sounds more like what you'd say to your horse than something a woman in distress wants to hear.

She drew in a breath, her eyes searching his. "You know my fiancé and I broke up last winter."

"You mentioned that. Are you getting back together with him?"

She shook her head. "No. But I've let my family—and probably you, too—assume that I initiated the breakup."

Brett tilted his head, not understanding.

"I didn't break up with him. He broke up with me because—" She took a shuddering breath, an almost pleading gaze fixed on him. "Because…I can't have children."

For a flashing moment, he thought his heart stopped beating. He hadn't seen that one coming.

"Aww, babe." Stunned at her words and the sorrow in her eyes, he pulled her to him and she came willingly to be cradled in his arms. She had all that pain bottled up inside and he'd been playing the clown when she tried to tell him. When would he ever learn?

He held her trembling body as she wept. Not violent, racking sobs, but a muted variety, as if she'd already used up her tear supply and was now down to the final dregs. *Show me how to respond, Lord.* Her tears dampened his shirt as he laid his head against her hair, tightening his arms more securely around her.

No, he hadn't seen that one coming.

But it explained so much. The sadness he'd picked up on the first day he'd met her. The unexpected silences. The wistfulness in her eyes when around Jori. How she sometimes ran hot and cold with him.

"I'm sorry, Abby."

She nodded acknowledgment of his words, her tears coming even more softly now. He reached into his back pocket for a handkerchief and slipped it into the hand curled at his chest. She turned slightly away and blew her nose. A sound so dainty that under other circumstances he'd have been tempted to laugh.

"You're going to be okay," he assured, brushing her hair back in a motion intended to sooth. But what a tragic disappointment for a young woman who'd wanted someday to have a family. For her to be rejected by her fiancé for that very reason made his blood boil.

His jaw hardened. What a jerk.

She pulled back slightly and looked up at him, then dropped her gaze to dab at her eyes with a corner of the handkerchief. "I'm sorry for being such a blubber baby."

He tilted her chin toward him. "Don't apologize. You have every right to cry."

She brushed at his shirt. "I've soaked you."

"It'll dry."

"I…I've never told anyone but my mom—and recently Meg—that Gene was the one who broke up with me. Or the reason why. Not even my dad."

"Why not?"

"I didn't want anyone feeling sorry for me. This is a happy time with Jori's arrival. I didn't want to ruin it."

"So you've been dealing with it all on your own."

"For the past five months. Just me and God, even though I've sometimes left Him out of the equation." She dabbed at her eyes again. "It hasn't been the easiest thing coming to Canyon Springs and being recruited to look after Davy and teach Sunday school. Now there's Jori in the house."

No wonder she'd been desperate to get out of town. It hadn't been all about running from the difficulties with her dad.

"Gene and I got engaged at Thanksgiving and were planning a June wedding. My previous doctor had just retired, so during winter break I went in for a physical with a new one in preparation of—" she blushed and lowered her head "—you know, for getting married. That's when I found out. Test after confirming test."

"There's nothing…?"

"No, nothing that can be fixed." She swallowed hard, still avoiding his gaze. "I saw more specialists than I can count. You see, it's just that—"

He slipped his finger under her chin and raised her face to his. "You don't have to explain the details, Abby. I understand."

She gave him a faint, grateful smile. "I knew Gene wanted children. But I hadn't expected that I wouldn't be able to fulfill my part of the bargain."

Brett frowned. "Is that what he told you? That you weren't fulfilling your commitment?"

She nodded. "But I'd rather have him be honest than marry me and be unhappy the rest of his life. He'd been a widower a number of years. Why should I hold him back from having children when he can still have them with someone else?"

"I may be old-fashioned, but usually a man wants children to be the offspring of a woman he loves."

"*Usually* being the operative word here." She gave him a sad smile. "Now that I can look at the situation more objectively, I think he thought at age forty that the timing was right to get married again and start a family."

"And you happened to be in the neighborhood?" A growing heaviness settled in Brett's chest. This was why she'd shied away from him all along, correctly perceiving he wanted children. That's why she bolted when he kissed her today.

"I'm sorry, Abby. I know this came as a blow. A heartbreaker. You've got to know, though, that none of this will matter to the right man."

But was *he* that man? Or was he every bit the same jerk as her ex-fiancé?

"I wish…" She gave a soft sigh that cracked open his heart. "I wish I could understand why I can't have children. I don't mean the medical reasons. I know that clearly enough. But I wish I understood God's plan. Why He gave me a longing for kids and then an inability to have any."

Her pain was almost tangible, but he was helpless to make it go away.

"Sometimes things just happen." His words came softly. "Our bodies, like this decaying world, are imperfect. It has nothing to do with us doing anything wrong and being punished or other people doing anything right and getting the same things *we* want."

How often he'd been over that ground after losing Jeremy. It had taken him a long time to shake off the fear that his own shortcomings, his earlier lack of faith in God, had meant God had to take Jeremy away from him to get his attention.

It was only years later that he could better accept that Jeremy's genetically weakened lungs hadn't been capable of weathering the pneumonia. It wasn't a punishment. God loved him and Jeremy and Melynda. While not a good thing in and of itself, God nevertheless brought about good things through Jeremy's illness. Like bringing his daddy closer to Him.

Should he share that with Abby now? About his journey?

He gazed into her tear-streaked face. No, now wasn't the time. It would appear to diminish her own grief. Appear to belittle it, and he couldn't do that. Her heartache was every bit as devastating as his, but in a different way.

He brushed Abby's hair back from her face. "I wish I had answers for you, Abby. But sometimes there aren't any. At least none that satisfy, and certainly none that satisfy so soon after being dealt such a blow."

"Like when your wife left you?"

And losing Jeremy.

"Yes. While I've mostly come to terms with it, I don't understand it. But I'm more sorry than words can express that you're having to go through this, Abby. I've seen you with Davy and Jori and there's no doubt you'd make a loving mom."

But her revelation put a whole new spin on things for him....

That evening Abby sat alone on the darkened front porch. Joe was working and Meg, Davy and Jori had gone to a barbecue and baby shower held by her friends from school. Abby had been invited along, but she'd hoped Brett might call. Or stop by.

Which was foolish thinking on her part.

He'd responded gallantly to her tears and did his best to comfort her. He'd said all the right things and it had felt so good, so right, to be held by him. His strength encompassed and reassured her. He'd gone through a divorce, but could he really understand the depths of pain, disappointment and anger she'd experienced these past months? How she felt somehow cheated, as if being forced to repay a debt she didn't owe?

She reached for the light sweater she'd learned to keep nearby in the high country, even in summer, and draped it over her shoulders to ward off the chill that had come on the heels of sunset.

Brett said her childlessness wouldn't matter to the right man, but despite the earlier kiss and the growing feelings between them, she'd been right. Her situation was a deal breaker for any man who wanted children, just as it had been for Gene.

If there was any blessing in the timing of learning that she couldn't have kids it was that it happened before she'd married her fiancé. What a mistake that would have been. Not only would he have resented her when the discovery was later made, but in the past week she'd come to realize that she'd been drawn to him because of what she'd perceived as his stability. Dependability. Security.

How had she not recognized earlier that the separation from her father at age ten had instilled in her a classic need for someone to fill that male parent role? Gene, twelve years older, had been well established in his academic profession. Steady. Reliable. A father figure. It seemed so clear now.

God was to be the source of her security, not any man.

The phone in her pocket chimed. *Please let it be Brett.*

But it was her brother Ed, checking in to see when she might be coming back to Tucson. They chatted a few minutes, with her filling him in on baby Jori and him expressing surprise that she'd applied for a position in Canyon Springs.

It *was* pretty crazy. Brett initially seemed as excited as she was that she'd be staying in town if she got the job. But how did he feel now that he knew the truth about her? Was he still praying she'd get the job, or had he abandoned that prayer request immediately? Should she withdraw her application?

She closed her eyes and gently rocked in the porch swing, her thoughts drifting to those laughing moments when she'd snatched Brett's hat and he'd pursued. How they'd ended up in each other's arms. And now, reliving how his lips had so gently caressed hers...

She could even smile at the good-natured ribbing by the cowboy-hatted teens. They liked Brett and obviously had fun with him. Old dude, they'd taunted, as if he'd long ridden over the hill.

It had been fun, exhilarating, during that brief instant in his arms to let her imagination run free. To feel hope that, even if only during those fleeting moments, a man like Brett might be able to care for her—and commit to her—in spite of everything.

She knew in her heart of hearts that she might not see him again. Or if she did, it might only be a time for him, decent man that he was, to give them both closure, to let her down gently. But was she giving up too easily? Could Brett, right this very minute, be communing with their God, asking Him what path he was to take? Meg had been so certain that he cared for her, that adoption wouldn't be an unrealistic option to fulfill his dreams of fatherhood.

How fortunate any child—biological or otherwise—would be to call Brett dad.

Rising from the porch swing, Abby moved to sit on the railing and gazed out on the windless night. Up and down the street interior lights glowed a welcome reassurance and ponderosa branches arched protectively overhead. Somehow, God felt so very close. Watching over her. Filling her with peace.

She'd always heard that prayers that aren't prayed will never be answered…and in so many subtle ways Brett had played a role in reawakening her faith.

"Father God," she murmured softly, lifting her face to the star-filled night. "Is there still any chance for me and Brett?"

"And even knowing what you know about her now, you still haven't told Abby about Jeremy, have you?"

Geri seemed more irritated with him than usual as he poured a mug of coffee Thursday morning, then lowered himself into an easy chair in front of the fireplace. Soft light filtered in around the curtains, heralding another new day.

He hadn't slept much last night and had seriously considered not picking up his sister's call. He might just hang up if she asked him if he'd care to share. He had more than enough on his mind. Work. Nailing down a physician for the kids' camp. And figuring out what he was going to do about Abby.

Yesterday had been a game changer.

Making a decision about whether or not to have kids was no longer theoretical, and it was eating him up in a way he'd never have expected.

"It wouldn't have been right to tell her when her heart's breaking over the inability to have children and the fact that a former fiancé dumped her for that very reason. It would have been insensitive, like I was trying to diminish her own loss."

Geri was silent for a moment. "When she shared that with you, how did you respond?"

He set the steaming mug of coffee on a nearby coaster. "As best I could."

"You didn't tell her kids don't make the marriage?"

"I told her it wouldn't matter to the right man."

Geri gave an exasperated sigh. "But you didn't use that opportunity to tell her you were the right man? Good going, Brett."

"I'm not going to lie and say I haven't come to care deeply for Abby." He reached again for the mug, clasping it between his hands as her gentle smile came vividly to mind. "But you know I've always wanted kids, even after losing Jeremy and knowing the risks involved in possibly having another child with CF."

"You can always adopt. Don't tell me a Marden hasn't thought of that option."

"Believe me, I've gone the rounds with that one ever since Abby told me. But after Melynda remarried, I've been believing that when the time is right, God will bring a woman into my life with whom I'll be able to have kids, just like you and Mike. Like all my brothers and sisters."

"You prayed you'd fall in love with someone who wasn't a CF carrier."

"Right."

"Well, it looks like your prayer was answered, baby brother."

It had been. So why couldn't he accept that with a grateful heart? Thank God for lifting the cystic fibrosis burden? Thank Him for bringing Abby into his life?

"It sounds," his sister continued, "as if having biological kids is more important than you realized. But you know what? The fact that you're struggling with this tells me you're coming to love Abby or this wouldn't be a struggle at all. You'd move on and keep praying for another woman."

"I guess so."

"Brett?"

"Yeah?"

"Just let me say this and then I'll shut up. Don't wait too long to make up your mind. You know Mom always says not making a decision is in essence making a decision."

And not making a decision to be willing to adopt was to decide to let Abby go.

Chapter Seventeen

She looks a lot like you did at that age. Dad's words echoed in Abby's ears late Thursday afternoon.

Gazing down at Jori in her arms, she gently swayed her to the motion of the rocker she'd given Joe and Meg a few nights ago. Her sister-in-law was taking a much-needed nap before suppertime. Despite avoiding the infant as much as possible this past week, when Jori had awakened fussing Abby had done the only thing she knew to do to keep from disturbing an exhausted Meg—pick the baby up and hold her.

Jori's tiny fingers now wrapped around a single one of Abby's, drawing it to her mouth, her big dark eyes solemnly studying Abby's. *Did* her niece look like Abby had at that age? What would it have been like to have a little girl like this to call her own?

With a heavy heart, Abby drew in the soothing scent of sun-warmed pine drifting through the open windows of the living room. All was quiet except for an occasional vehicle passing by or the twitter of sparrows. Lulled by the late afternoon sounds and scents, she closed her eyes. She'd always dreamed of being a stay-at-home mom. That was one reason she'd chosen her librarian degree with the background of teaching, planning to be off during the summers and school breaks right along with her school-age children.

What if this were her little house in Canyon Springs? This baby hers? Her imagination floated onward, picturing her husband arriving home to stand in the doorway observing them. She could almost feel his gaze upon her and envision how she'd look up and smile. He'd smile back, telling her how beautiful mother and daughter looked. How blessed he was. They'd gaze down at their child, a perfect blend of both of them, her black hair...and eyes that captured her daddy's secret smile.

Abby drew a sharp breath and sat up straighter, belatedly realizing that from the moment her make-believe husband had stepped into the daydream house, he'd morphed into Brett Marden. Sadness washed over her as she shifted the now-sleeping Jori in her arms. She would have no children. Not with Brett. Not with anyone.

She hadn't seen Brett since her meltdown after the kiss. Not so much as a phone call. She'd really thought she'd hear from him. Or rather, she'd prayed she would. That evening on the front porch she'd felt such a sense of assurance, of hope, that God would work things out. But it wasn't to be.

She again gazed down at her niece's tiny face. So sweet. But why didn't God want *her* to have a child of her own? And why did the man her heart longed for have to be so blatantly dad material?

"So how's our little pumpkin today?" a familiar male voice cheerfully questioned from the front door.

Startled, Abby looked to where Brett stood on the porch, his hands cupped to peer in through the screen door. Why hadn't she heard his approach? How long had he been standing there?

Heart beating a ramped-up cadence, she nodded to the little one. "She's sleeping."

"Oh, sorry." He put his finger to his lips. "Shhhh."

Then he opened the screen door and stepped inside with the table he'd refinished to match the rocker. He set it on the floor, then pulled off his hat and quietly approached to stand looking down at them.

"You two are beautiful there like that, almost like a painting with the late afternoon light filtering from the windows."

Abby swallowed, the parallel to her daydream not lost on her.

He motioned to the table. "I was in the neighborhood, so wanted to drop this off for Meg. Is she around?"

"She's napping. Totally exhausted. That's why I have Jori. She was fussy and I was afraid she'd wake her mommy."

"You have her quieted down now." He squatted next to them, then reached out to brush the back of his fingers across the child's smooth cheek. So gentle. Paternal. "Your rocker must have done the trick."

"Seems to."

He stood again, fiddling with the hat in his hand, his eyes boring uncertainly into hers. "So…how are you?"

He meant, no doubt, how was she after she'd poured out all her grief on him, soaked him with her tears. Should she apologize? Make light of it?

"I'm good."

"I know it has to be rough." He nodded toward Jori, remembering she'd told him it wasn't easy being around her niece and nephew.

"It will get better."

He nodded again and glanced at the door. But she didn't want him to go. Not yet.

"The table you refinished is beautiful. Meg will love it."

"You think so?" He brought it over to place it by the rocker. "Pretty good match, huh?"

"It is. No one would ever guess they weren't a set." Sort of how the secondhand shop owner thought she and Brett went together. But she wouldn't say that aloud. The man had been mistaken.

Brett glanced toward the door again, shuffled his feet. Then to her surprise, he turned to her with hope-filled eyes. "I, uh, guess what I really came over here for was to see if—"

"Brett! What are you doing here?"

A sleepy-eyed Meg came slowly down the stairs. She wasn't quite up to dashing up and down them yet, and kept a hand on the railing to steady herself.

But what had Brett been about to say?

"I brought a baby gift." He motioned to the table beside him. "A match to Abby's rocker."

"Ohhh." Meg's face crumpled as she crossed the floor to gaze down at the little table. Then she turned to Brett and gave him a hug. "You sweetheart, you. I love it."

"We matched the finishes," Abby added, not taking her eyes off Brett's face. He'd looked at her with hope in his eyes, hadn't he? Not sorrow or regret. There had even been a trace of twinkle in his eyes if she hadn't been mistaken. Could that mean...?

Her spirits skyrocketed.

No, no, don't read something into this just yet. Not yet.

"You're welcome to stay for dinner, Brett," Meg offered. "Abby put a roast and potatoes in the slow cooker, thinking it wouldn't warm the house too much on a summer day."

"I smelled it the moment I stepped in the door." He glanced almost anxiously at Abby, then his mouth twisted in regret. "But I'm afraid I can't stay."

Stay, stay. Abby hoped the expression in her eyes conveyed that to him. But he placed his hat on his head.

"Mom?" Davy called from the patio door. "Camy's found something stinky and I can't get her to drop it."

Meg shook her head. "Thanks so much for the table, Brett. We'll cherish it." Then she hurried to the back of the house.

Abby's gaze met Brett's as he moved toward the door. "I'll see you out."

She quickly rose to place the sleeping Jori in her bassinet, then followed him as he stepped out onto the porch.

What had he been going to say?

He squinted, gazing off down the street for a long moment, then back at her, his expression now hesitant as he lowered his voice. "How would you like to go out to dinner tomorrow night?"

He was asking her out? She couldn't suppress a smile. "I'd like that. A lot."

"We could go to Kit's," he elaborated, "then maybe out to the property where the kids' camp will be held. I can show you around."

"That would be nice. I'd like to see it. You've found a doctor, then?"

His brow lowered. "Not yet. But we're waiting on a few callbacks."

"Good." That let her off the hook.

A smile again tugged at his lips. "I'll pick you up at six, if that's okay."

"I'm looking forward to it."

He studied her a moment, the expression in his eyes suddenly serious. Before she knew what he intended to do, he leaned in for a quick kiss on her cheek. Then headed down the porch steps.

"We sure hate to lose Brett around here." From where she and her daughter sat on Singing Rock lodge's front steps Friday afternoon, Olivia's mouth took a downward turn. "We've come to count on him."

Brett was leaving town? He'd decided to return to Phoenix? The ranch? "Why are you losing him?"

Olivia made a face. "That no-good Trey Kenton talked him into joining up with the High Country Equine Center as a full-time assistant manager. So now we have to find someone else to be on call here at night."

Abby relaxed, the feelings that had been cruising at a ridiculously high altitude since last evening taking off once again. He wasn't leaving town after all.

"I hadn't heard that."

"Brett told Rob just this morning, so it hasn't had time to get around town yet." Olivia scooped Angie into her lap. "Thanks again for dropping off the empty dish. I'm glad Joe and Davy enjoyed the lasagna."

Thank goodness Olivia hadn't brought enchiladas.

Abby glanced toward Brett's cabin, noting an unfamiliar pickup parked in front of it. "Brett has company?"

"His twin sisters. But he doesn't know it yet. They arrived a while ago to surprise him for his birthday." It was Brett's birthday? "I let them in when they promised nothing malicious was intended."

"I'd love to meet his sisters." But arriving on his doorstep when he wasn't there could prove awkward. Require explanation.

"They're nice," Olivia prompted. "Red-haired dynamos, exactly like Brett's always described. You should go over and introduce yourself. You'll get a kick out of meeting them just like I did."

Abby glanced again at the cabin. What would it hurt? "Maybe I'll pop in for a few minutes to say hello."

Saying goodbye to Olivia, Abby headed to the cabin. As she stepped up onto the porch, she could hear the cheery chatter of female voices inside. Would she see any resemblance to Brett? Find any similarities in mannerisms? Expressions?

Gingerly, she knocked on the wood-framed screen door. Almost instantly a perky, red-haired woman in her mid-thirties appeared in the doorway, a welcoming smile on her face.

"Hello, whoever you are. Brett's not here right now, but I'm his sister Erin."

"Hi, Erin. I'm Abby Diaz, a friend of—"

"Abby? You're Abby?"

The excitement in the voice of another woman coming up behind Erin was unmistakable. She eagerly pushed open the screen door. No doubt about it, the two were twins. Dark brown eyes, freckles, bright red hair swept up into ponytails and identical mile-wide smiles. Thank goodness they were wearing different colored tops or they'd be impossible to tell apart

"I'm Geri. Erin and I've been dying to meet you. Come on in."

Brett had told them about her?

Abby stepped hesitantly inside and a tan-and-black terrier that could probably fit neatly inside Elmo's mouth trotted across the hardwood floor, barking shrilly.

Erin turned to scoop it up and tuck it under her arm. "Now hush, Fergie. This is your uncle Brett's girlfriend. Isn't she pretty?"

Uncle Brett? Wonder what he thought of that?

And girlfriend? Did they know something she didn't? A ripple of anticipation danced up her spine. Had he identified her to his sisters that way—a woman he'd known barely two weeks—or had they jumped to conclusions?

"You're scaring her, Erin," Geri warned as she studied Abby with anxious eyes. Then she flashed a reassuring smile. "We're harmless, Abby. Honest. We're just excited to meet you. Brett hasn't dated anyone in, well, next to forever."

She'd hardly call them dating, but something had led

them to think that. Could Brett be further along in thinking about their relationship than she'd assumed?

Erin nodded. "We've prayed so long and so hard for a
special woman for our little brother. He's one of the great-
est guys we've ever known. But after Melynda left him,
he's dragged his feet."

"Can I get you something to drink?" Geri asked.
"Water? Soda?"

"No, thank you. I can't stay long. Olivia McGuire—
she's my cousin—just mentioned you were here and encouraged me to stop in and say hello."

Geri clasped her hands to her chest, her gaze devour-
ing Abby as enthusiastically as that of her sister. "This is
so exciting."

Okaaaay. She'd take her word for it. But Abby couldn't
help feeling anticipation building inside. Brett wanted to
see her tonight. What about?

"I knew the first time he called and mentioned you and
that banana with legs and how you captivated the kindergarteners with a Bible story, that he saw something special in you."

"I knew something was up," Erin chimed in, "when genetic matches started weighing on his mind."

Genetic matches?

"Melynda just couldn't handle it," Geri clarified, sadness clouding her eyes. "When she called it quits, he re-
treated from the world for years. Buried himself in his
work."

"I think," Erin said quietly, "that losing Jeremy has
played a big part in it, too."

Jeremy?

Erin's expression softened further. "He was the sweet-
est little guy, Abby. You'd have loved him."

What was she saying? That Brett and Melynda had a
son and she'd taken him away when she'd divorced him?

Just like Abby's mother had done? Why hadn't Brett told her this?

Geri nodded, her smile tinged with sorrow. "He's missed his boy so much."

"What happened?" Abby looked from one sister to the other. "Did Melynda get sole custody?"

Is that why he'd never mentioned a child? The separation was too painful to talk about?

As if frozen, the twins stared blankly at her. Then exchanged an uneasy glance.

"Brett still hasn't told you?" Geri ventured cautiously.

Abby shook her head. "Told me what?"

What was going on? The pair exchanged looks again, then Erin nodded to her sister as if giving her the go-ahead.

"I don't know how to say this, Abby. Or even if I should."

What was the big mystery? Surely Brett hadn't done anything so awful that warranted being legally banned from his son.

"Jeremy…" Geri took a deep breath, her troubled gaze probing Abby's. "Jeremy died when he was five. We thought you knew."

Ice-cold fingers gripped Abby's throat.

Brett had a son and that son was dead.

Her legs weakened and for a moment she thought she might faint. In desperation, she looked from one twin to the other, her voice faltering.

"What…what happened?"

Geri's eyes pierced into hers. "Quick, Erin, get her a chair. And something to drink."

Abby gratefully lowered herself into the kitchen chair, but waved away the water. "Brett had a son who died? What happened?"

"I feel so awful." Erin moved to her side. "I thought Brett told you by now. He said he was going to do it yesterday. He'd even asked us to pray."

Yesterday. Is that why he'd come by the house?

She shook her head slowly. They were to have dinner together tonight, then go out to the site of the kids' camp. From the look in his eyes, she'd hoped it was the beginning of good things. Getting to know each other better. But in retrospect, remembering Brett's abrupt sobering just before he kissed her cheek, this was to have been a part of that. Telling her about his boy.

"What happened?" Abby repeated. Was no one going to tell her?

"Complications," Geri said, eyeing her uneasily, "from cystic fibrosis."

Cystic fibrosis. The same genetic disease Janet Logan's grandson had. Brett's son had it, too?

"I really wish you could be hearing this from Brett." Geri's lips tightened. "Jeremy's lungs were already weakened from the disease. And when he caught a bad cold and cough, it progressed almost overnight into pneumonia. A snowstorm swept in and they couldn't get him from the ranch to a hospital in time to save him."

Trembling deep inside, Abby sat speechless. Brett. A son.

She closed her eyes as memory flashed to the day she'd confessed her inability to have children. Brett had held her in his arms and consoled her. He'd listened as the pain had erupted from inside. Dried tears. Comforted.

And yet…he'd lost a child of his own.

Not a hoped-for, dreamed-of child of his imagination, but a flesh and blood one. A son he'd held in his arms and into whose eyes he'd gazed. A little boy who would have smiled back and called him daddy.

"Abby? Are you okay?" Geri's voice came as if from a galaxy far away.

"I'm…okay." But the icy coldness persisted and the depth of her trembling intensified. Shock? With a sense of dread, she directed her gaze to the framed photos on the fireplace mantel. Was Jeremy here among the smiling faces of his many cousins? How had she missed him when she'd been here before?

She managed to rise on shaky legs, then haltingly approached the mantel to scan the photographed faces. Why hadn't Brett pointed him out to her?

"Which one?"

Sensing the twins' hesitation, she turned to where they stood staring at her with distraught eyes. She swallowed back the lump forming in her throat. "Which one?"

"The little guy on the far right," Erin confirmed with obvious reluctance, her voice small. "With the cowboy hat."

Abby moved in closer, gripping the mantel's edge to steady herself as she focused on a five-by-seven professional studio portrait. That one hadn't been there before. Had Brett deliberately removed it when he'd insisted she give him a few minutes to run inside and tidy up?

Why?

With tremulous hands, she lifted down the photo of a sweet-faced boy who sported his daddy's smile.

Jeremy. Brett's son.

"He never said a word," she said softly, tears pricking her eyes. Did he think so little of her, that he couldn't bring himself to share this life-impacting loss?

Geri came to stand by her, looking down at the photograph. "I'm sure he was waiting for the right time, Abby. He cares for you. I'm sure of it. That's why Erin and I—" She turned her gaze to her sister in appeal. "From what Brett had said about you, we—"

"What Geri means," Erin said, coming to join them, "is that we know our brother well enough to recognize he's crazy about you."

A soft sound of distress escaped Abby's lips. She shook

her head as her finger traced the boy's dimple that was just like his father's. She'd carried on awful about her loss, her disappointment, her anger and inability to understand why God had allowed her dream of being a mother to be snatched away. Yet all that time Brett harbored unimaginable wounds of his own. Wounds so raw and so deep he couldn't even tell her about them.

What must he think of her? Of her poor, pitiful, it's-all-about-me outpouring? Is that why he hadn't shared this part of his life? He thought she was incapable of compassion? That she had nothing to offer him, nothing to help him heal?

"Don't be mad at him, Abby. Please." Geri slipped an arm around her waist. "He's seldom talked to anyone outside the family about Jeremy, but I'm so certain he's at that point with you that I fully thought he already had. He was supposed to have told you yesterday."

Abby shook her head. "You don't understand."

"I understand he's coming to love you. That he's likely dreaming of—"

"A replacement for his son?" Abby snapped, the bitterness in her response unmistakable.

Geri stepped back, releasing Abby. "No, not a replacement. Of course not. Jeremy can never be replaced, but—"

"Thank you for telling me about him." With trembling fingers Abby set the frame firmly back on the mantel, the boy's smile burning into her heart. She had to get out of here, get away from Brett's stricken-looking sisters, who were clearly appalled they'd divulged his secret. A secret he hadn't felt he could share with *her*.

"What are you going to do?" Erin nibbled on her lower lip, her eyes anxious. "Brett's not going to be happy with us. We didn't mean to break a confidence, to tell you before he had a chance to. Please don't let this cause a rift between you."

She didn't know what she was going to do, except that she couldn't let things go any further with Brett than they already had.

Geri touched her arm. "I know he's taking special care with the way he wants to tell you about his son."

Abby moved to the door and stepped out onto the porch, the sisters following her.

"We're so sorry," Geri whispered. "Please forgive us."

"There's nothing to forgive. It's not your fault."

It was hers, for selfishly wanting to believe God had a plan for her and Brett as a couple, that the born-to-be-a-dad Brett Marden should give up his dreams of family in exchange for loving her.

Chapter Eighteen

"So you're telling Abby tonight?" Janet Logan handed the box of name tags across the kitchen table to Brett. As a step of faith, with only a few days remaining before the camp would have to be called off for lack of an on-site doctor, they'd begun filling welcome packets that afternoon. He had one more physician to hear back from. Dr. Wylie in Flagstaff.

"Yep, tonight's the night."

"To tell her about Jeremy *and*…?"

"Yep, *and*."

Once he'd come to a firm decision—he still couldn't understand why it had been such a struggle—he'd sought her out late yesterday afternoon hoping to find time alone with her. He'd even put his sisters on prayer alert. But Meg had interrupted and it appeared Abby was in charge of supper preparations, so it hadn't been a good time to steal away with her.

But tonight he intended to put into no uncertain terms—no clowning around—what his feelings were for her. He'd tell her right up front that he was the man to whom her childlessness didn't matter. And whether or not she chose to stay in Canyon Springs, he wanted to keep in touch in hopes that perhaps over time…

It was a bold, crazy move to make any way you looked at it. They'd met barely two weeks ago and Trey would probably never let him hear the end of it. But he couldn't let her walk out of his life without her knowing how he felt. Without telling her about Jeremy.

Janet slid a camp schedule into one of the nine-by-twelve envelopes. "You haven't known each other long, but it's clear you've come to care for her. Getting this out in the open where it can be discussed will be a burden off your shoulders and may lead the way to an understanding between the two of you."

"That's what I'm praying for." He handed her a box of camp key chains. "But even having the door slammed in my face will be better than a lifetime of wondering if I should have spoken up."

"With the exception of anything to do with Melynda and Jeremy, speaking up has been who you are. The fact that you've been reticent when it comes to matters of the heart tells me you think an awful lot of this young woman."

"I do. I hope she takes me seriously."

Janet gave him a disbelieving look. "Why wouldn't she?"

"I get the feeling she doesn't entirely approve of what she perceives as my lighthearted approach to life."

"You've had more than your share of serious in this world and, once she knows about Jeremy, Abby will come to understand that." She slipped a schedule into another envelope. "There's no shame in living out the joy God puts before us. Rejecting it wouldn't honor Jeremy's memory. Or God."

Brett rubbed his hand along the back of his neck. "Life hasn't turned out the way I'd have chosen, but I have a lot to be thankful for. In spite of everything, I can't imagine not ever having had Jeremy in my life."

"When will you see Abby?"

"I told her I'd pick her up at six." Two hours from now. The beginning or the end.

"I'll be praying."

Brett reached for another envelope just as his cell phone vibrated. He unclipped it from his belt to look at the caller ID, then his gaze locked with Janet's.

"It's Dr. Wylie."

Heart still hammering, Abby pulled her car up outside her brother's house and turned off the engine. Wiped away tears. She had to pull herself together, gather her stuff, pack the car and get as far away from Canyon Springs as possible. But the minute she set foot in the door, Meg would know something was wrong.

What would Brett think if she wasn't here when he arrived tonight? She had no doubt he planned to tell her about Jeremy this evening. But whether it was to clarify why, despite earlier evidence to the contrary, he couldn't move forward with their relationship or if it was to assure her that having biological children wasn't important to him, she didn't know.

All she knew was that she couldn't let him make that sacrifice.

She'd known all along that Brett deserved a big happy family like the one he'd grown up in. She cared for him too much to expect him to give that up for her.

Tears pricked her eyes anew.

She didn't know how long she'd been sitting there, staring out into space, when a sharp rapping sound came at the car's rolled-up passenger-side window, startling Abby.

"What are you doing sitting out here?" Meg, with Jori in her arms, frowned her concern. "What's wrong?"

Should she tell her? Was it really hers to tell about Jeremy if Brett had chosen not to make it widely known?

She'd already unwittingly disclosed the news of his divorce.

She stepped quickly from the car to face her sister-in-law. "I'm feeling a little emotional, I guess. I've decided to head home tonight."

"Only temporarily, right?" Meg studied her closely. "Not permanently."

Abby shrugged, forcing a smile. "Canyon Springs was a nice dream, but it's not where I belong. I need to get back to my real life."

"But what about the job? Working things out with your dad?"

"The timing's not really right."

Meg shifted Jori in her arms, her eyes narrowing. "This is about Brett, isn't it? What happened? What did he do? Did you have a fight?"

"No, nothing like that. But it's complicated. I don't think I'm up to untangling it for you right now. I need some time to sort things out."

"You'd better tell me, or I'm going to call Brett and give him a piece of my mind."

Abby skirted around the front of the car to join her sister-in-law. "Please don't. None of this is his fault. It's just time for me to go."

"This makes no sense."

Abby looked toward the house. "Is Davy here? I'd like to say goodbye to him. Then gather my things and pop over and see Dad."

"You're serious, aren't you? You're really leaving right now. But weren't you thinking about helping at the kids' camp? And Davy was looking forward to going horseback riding with you and Brett."

"Brett will still take him riding and I'm sure there will be plenty of volunteers for the camp. And don't forget,

Meg, there's no guarantee I'll be offered the librarian position."

"Joe is not going to be happy about this."

"I'll come visit once in a while. Besides, nothing's stopping him from coming to Tucson. The road is navigable from both directions."

"I'm so disappointed, Abby." Meg shifted Jori again. "I thought for sure you and Brett—"

"Me, too." She drew a slow breath, feeling more in control now that she'd come to a decision. She'd be back in Tucson not long after dark. Back in her own bed. Back to all that was familiar and well-ordered.

She could only hope and pray that losing Brett wouldn't haunt her for the rest of her life.

"She what?" Brett stood on the front porch of the Diaz home, dressed in his Sunday best, a bouquet of mixed flowers clenched in his hand.

"Just like I said," Meg stated, her tone abnormally cool. "She left for Tucson a few hours ago."

"Why?"

"You tell me." From the folded arms and the disapproving look on her face, Meg held him at fault.

"If I knew, do you think I'd be standing here holding these?" He shook the flowers at her.

"You would be if you had an apology to make."

What had he done? Abby said she was looking forward to tonight. She'd looked pretty happy about it, too. "What did she say when she left?"

"She said Canyon Springs was nothing but a nice dream."

He frowned. "They turned her down already for that librarian job?"

"Not yet."

His grip tightened on the flowers. "This doesn't make any sense. That's *all* she said?"

"When I asked her if the two of you had argued, she said no, but that it was complicated and she didn't feel like discussing it."

He tipped his hat back on his head. "I don't know what to make of this. I haven't talked to Abby since yesterday when I was over here. We didn't have a fight. In fact, I was to pick her up and take her out to eat this evening. Which is why I'm standing on your doorstep dodging the daggers in your eyes."

Meg studied him skeptically, weighing his words. "Men can be so clueless."

"This one sure is. Give me a break here. In case you haven't noticed, I think Abby's a pretty special woman. I have no idea what I did to make her take off like this."

Meg's brow wrinkled. "You *sound* sincere."

"I am." Why would Abby have taken off without telling him? "You said she left a couple of hours ago to head straight down the mountain?"

"Maybe not straight down," Meg clarified. "I think she planned to see her dad on the way out of town."

His heart jumped. "She might still be there."

He could still catch her. Find out what was going on.

"She could be, I suppose, but—"

"Thanks, Meg, I'm on my way." He spun on a booted heel and headed down the porch steps just as his phone vibrated. He halted at the bottom of the stairs, hopes rising. Abby?

No, Geri.

"Hey, sis, what's up?" His words were clipped. He didn't have time for a leisurely chat with his sibling tonight.

"Brett?" his sister said cautiously, her voice void of its usual vibrant ring. "Erin and I spent the afternoon out at your place, waiting for you to come home."

"You're in Canyon Springs?" He glanced back at Meg, who was still watching him from the doorway. "What for?"

"A surprise. For your birthday."

With his anticipation of meeting with Abby, he'd forgotten it was his day to celebrate for another reason. But his sister's tone didn't sound happy birthdayish and he could hear an irritating little dog yapping in the background. Fergie, his niece.

"I wish I'd known you were coming." He glanced at his watch. "I'm sort of in the middle of something right now."

He could hear Geri in muffled conversation, as if she'd covered the mouthpiece to consult with her sister. Then she took a deep breath, her words hesitant. "We…met Abby."

They met Abby?

And now Abby was gone.

With a sinking feeling, he knew that could only mean one thing. "You told her about Jeremy."

A statement, not a question.

"You've seen her, then? Talked to her? Thank God." Geri's tone reflected her relief. "We thought you had already told her. You said you were going to, and she didn't seem surprised when we mentioned Melynda."

He closed his eyes momentarily, trying to get a grip on his emotions.

"No, I hadn't told her yet." Why had he kept putting it off? Not trusting God? Meg was right, this was all his fault.

"She seemed pretty upset," Geri ventured. "Is she okay now?"

He swallowed as he raised his eyes to the pines overhead. "I don't know. I haven't seen her. She left town."

Geri gasped. "She had plans to leave town?"

"Not that I knew of."

Again the sisters whispered between themselves. Then

Geri sighed deeply. "This is all our fault, Brett. We're so sorry."

A muscle tightened in his jaw. "Look, I can't talk now. I may still be able to catch her."

"You can? Then go. Go!"

"Wait. Where are you staying tonight? At my place?"

"Are you kidding?" He could envision Geri's lip curling at the thought of doubling up with her sister in his diminutive accommodations and him on the sofa. "We gave up waiting for you and are already at Nancy's Bed-and-Breakfast."

"Okay. Maybe I can catch you there later."

"Fine. Now go. Go!"

"I didn't want to leave without telling you, Dad." Abby stood at the side of the deck, gazing across the treed property of the Lazy D Campground and RV Park, her head pressed to her father's chest. It had felt good to tell him about her childlessness at last. To step into his arms and be held. Simply held. Just as she'd been when a little girl. A homecoming.

But she'd lingered here longer than she'd intended. Brett would be arriving anytime at Meg and Joe's place, discovering she'd left for Tucson.

"I'm sorry, honey."

She sighed and gave a halfhearted chuckle. "You may be stuck with me forever, Dad. Who's going to want me now?"

Did that sound pitiful or what?

"Now, now, none of that." He gave her another squeeze. "You're a wonderful woman any man in his right mind would thank God for giving him, kids or no kids."

She drew back slightly to look up at him. "The problem is, I'm falling in love with a man who is all about family."

"Brett Marden."

"You guessed?"

He smiled. "It's hard to overlook when two people light up when the other one walks into the room."

"He lights up, too?"

"Clearly."

A flash of hope snuffed out immediately. "But that doesn't change the fact that I can't give him what I know he wants most. Kids."

As briefly as she could, she filled him in on Brett's tragic loss of his wife and son.

"I have a feeling what Brett wants most, honey, is a woman who's open to being loved by him. One who loves God and will stand by his side through thick and thin. He doesn't seem like the type to seek out a relationship solely because he's ready to start a family and any woman will do. He's deeper than that."

"That's what I'd tried to convince myself of. I'd hoped God had a plan, but…"

"But the fact that he lost a son complicates things."

"If only he'd told me, thought enough of me to share that part of himself. It tells me he doesn't trust me."

"It can't have been easy to find an appropriate time to tell you. That's a deep, deep wound and not one to be shared lightly. I can't imagine losing you, Ed or Joe at *any* age. Kids aren't supposed to go before the mom and dad."

"No." With a heavy sigh, she stepped back to slip from the secure warmth of her father's embrace. "I'd better get going. I don't want to drive the whole way in the dark."

"Stay the night here and leave in the morning."

"No. I need to go now. The drive will help blow the cobwebs out of my brain. Give me some God time."

"Talk to Brett before you leave." It wasn't a suggestion, but a command.

"Why? Only to hear what I already know he has to say? That he's sorry for not telling me about Jeremy sooner, but there's no future for us? Or I'll have to tell him the same because I can't allow him to give up children for me? Either way you look at it, we're both going to get hurt."

"Maybe so. But, sweetheart, stay and see it through. Don't just walk away."

Was that a shimmer of tears in Dad's eyes?

A lump formed in her throat. Was she doing to Brett what her mother had done to Dad? What Melynda had done to him, too?

She slipped her arms around her father's neck and gave him a parting hug. "I love you, Dad, but I can't. I have to go."

Chapter Nineteen

He'd just missed her.

Heavyhearted, Brett backed his truck out of the space next to Bill's vehicle. He hadn't spoken to Abby's father but a few minutes, just long enough to know that despite Bill's urging, she'd made her decision to leave Canyon Springs.

To leave him.

I'm sorry, son. Bill's heartfelt words echoed in his ears as Brett pulled onto the blacktopped road and headed back to town.

She didn't have that much of a head start. He could probably catch up with Abby if he tried, rode the speedometer on the high side. But to what end? Even Bill hadn't urged him to go after her, a man who regretted not doing so himself those many years ago when his wife had abandoned him. Clearly, Bill could read the handwriting on the wall of his daughter's heart and couldn't offer Brett more than an apology on behalf of his youngest child.

Some birthday it had turned out to be.

Brett slammed a fist into the steering wheel. He'd waited long after Melynda's departure to step into relationship waters. He hadn't rushed out to replace her, but had taken time to search his heart, his behaviors, asking God to create a clean heart in him, to forgive him for anything he'd done or had not done that contributed to the breakdown of his marriage.

He'd waited patiently, expectantly, for God to lead, doing his best to enjoy life in the interim, dwelling as little as possible on the past. Most of all, he'd guarded his heart well.

Maybe too well.

Once in town, he glanced down a shady street to Nancy's Bed-and-Breakfast and saw Geri's truck parked outside. His sisters had come all this way to surprise him for a birthday he hadn't even remembered. They'd had to make arrangements for kid care and carve out the time and money to make the trip from Kingman. But somehow he couldn't bring himself to join them tonight. He'd call to let them know he was okay and would see them tomorrow, assuring them Abby's departure wasn't their fault.

It was his.

Right now, though, he wanted only to head home to Singing Rock, where at least Elmo would be happy to see him. Driving slowly with the windows down, he drank in the cool evening air as he watched the silhouetted pines flash by under the illumination of a rising moon. As much as he loved ponderosa pine country, at times they closed in on him, were too claustrophobic for a boy who'd grown up on the wide-open range. He longed to see the horizon, to watch the sun set in the far distance to the lowing of cattle, not bid the day an early farewell behind a bank of towering treetops.

Maybe it was time to think about returning to the ranch?

Once his obligations for the summer season were over, there wasn't much keeping him here. He didn't have to take that equine center position. Dr. Wylie had turned them down for the kids' camp. The physician regretted it, but it was a turndown nevertheless. So tomorrow he and

Janet would be making phone calls to a couple dozen disappointed parents and kids.

And with Abby leaving… He glanced at the somewhat bedraggled bouquet on the seat next to him.

Melynda. Now Abby.

"That's it, Lord," he said aloud. "Don't ask me to risk my heart again."

Abby had tucked her car discreetly off to one side of Singing Rock lodge's parking lot, relieved that the truck belonging to one of Brett's sisters was no longer there.

Brett had pulled up in front of his cabin ten minutes ago and remained in the truck's cab as the twilight deepened. What had he felt when Meg told him she'd left? Relief? Thankfulness that he didn't have to give up the hope of children of his own for her? Grateful that he didn't have to find the words to reject her for the same reason Gene had sent her on her way? Unlike Gene, though, Brett had a kind heart. It would hurt him to hurt her.

She wasn't quite sure why she'd lingered tonight, the windows of her car rolled down to let in a barely there breeze, except she wanted to tell Brett she'd garnered her courage and placed a call directly to Gene's sister—who was delighted at the possibility of joining the team of volunteers should Brett's other prospects fall through.

And besides, she reluctantly admitted, Dad was right. She couldn't walk out of Brett's life like Mom had walked out of Dad's, not even if she had to hear things she'd rather not hear and feel things her heart might not be able to bear. Say things that would wound her even more than they hurt Brett. Mostly she couldn't leave without sharing comforting words for his terrible loss. The blood of her mother might run through her veins, but she was a Diaz, too.

She had to see this through to the end.

She watched as Brett climbed out of the truck and set-

tled himself on the porch steps, as if loath to go inside.
She cringed inwardly. She couldn't approach him out here
in the open. What if Angie spied him and came running?
Or Rob and Olivia strolled over for a chat?

So she waited. Prayed. And watched as the blue sky
overhead deepened, giving life to the beginnings of a
starry host above.

*How, Lord, can I say a final goodbye to the man I've
come to love?*

At long last he rose, then walked to the far side of the
cabin with the same confident stride that had captured her
heart the first day she'd met him. Or was it a bit slower
tonight? More measured?

He didn't return.

But she waited, anticipating that the lights would soon
come on and she'd gather her courage to face him.

Minutes ticked by and the cabin remained dark. Where
had he gone? Reluctantly, she opened her car door and
stepped out, then picked her way in the dimming light
across the parking lot and up the stairs to his door. She
knocked softly.

Waited.

He'd still be on call at Singing Rock until the transi-
tion to the equine center was completed. He probably had
to give at least two weeks' notice, so maybe he'd walked
down the trail that looped through the property to check
on another of the cabins?

She glanced at her watch. He'd been gone almost half
an hour. She couldn't hang out here all night. Was God
telling her this wasn't a good idea? That she should give
herself more time? While she hated the thought of driving the winding mountain road at night, she could still be
home not too awfully long after midnight.

Resigned, she stepped off the porch and looked back
at the darkened cabin one more time. Using her key chain

flashlight, she navigated her way back to the car, then climbed in. With a sigh, she buckled her seat belt.

This wasn't how the day was supposed to have ended.

But just as she leaned forward to insert the key in the ignition, a muscular arm reached through the open driver's-side window and snagged it from her fingers.

"Going somewhere, ma'am?"

He heard Abby's quick intake of breath and, in the illumination of a three-quarter moon, his gaze locked with hers. Even in the fading light, he'd recognized her car when he'd driven into the parking lot. He'd waited in vain for her approach, then finally slipped around back to check on Elmo and to wait her out. Gather his thoughts. But he couldn't wait any longer.

"You met my sisters."

"I did."

"And they told you about Jeremy."

"They did."

"I'm sorry, Abby. I should have told you. I—"

Gazing up at him she motioned with her hand to cut him short. "I know now and that's all that matters. But I couldn't leave town without telling you how sorry I am."

That's why she'd delayed her exodus? To express her condolences?

"I had no idea, Brett," she continued, "that you lost a child. I can't even imagine the depths of your loss. How much you must miss him."

"I do miss the little guy." Would he ever not? And while watching videos of him brought a bittersweet healing, they were never easy to view. "He'd have been thirteen on his next birthday. That doesn't even seem real."

Three years after that he'd have been driving. Maybe dating.

"I don't see how you're able to hang out with kids now and cuddle babies the way you do."

She'd already shared with him how she struggled with that, knowing she'd never hold one of her own in her arms.

"I wasn't able to at first," he confessed. Those early years after losing Jeremy had been painfully hard. "After a particularly difficult holiday visit, with nieces and nephews climbing all over me and clamoring for me to play with them as I'd done in the past, I'd pretty much decided no more family gatherings."

"But you're still close to your family," she said softly. "You do go back to see everyone, don't you?"

"I do. But only because, on the drive back to Phoenix after that holiday, God impressed a Bible verse on my heart. 'Let the little children come to me and do not hinder them.'"

She nodded, recognizing the verse.

"I convinced myself it didn't apply to my situation. But it kept playing repeatedly in my mind. The next day, I stumbled across a passage in the book of Isaiah about God gathering His lambs in His arms and carrying them close to His heart. That had to be a coincidence, right? But the next morning my devotional guide pointed out that Jesus took children in His arms, laid His hands on them and blessed them."

"Three reminders in just a few days."

He nodded. "I knew God had to be trying to tell me something—that if Jesus took the children in His arms to bless them, how could I do any less? That was the turning point. Not an easy one or overnight. But a turning point."

She blinked back tears and his heart ached to hold her.

"God will help you find your turning point, too, Abby, if you let Him."

He motioned to the cabin. "It's cooling down out here with the sun setting. Do you want to go inside?"

"No, thank you." But she did reach for the door latch and step out of the car.

She was so beautiful, painted by the moonlight, her hair tumbling loosely over her shoulders. He cleared his throat. "My sisters were pretty torn up that they'd told you about Jeremy before I did."

"It was a shock." She leaned against the rear door of the car. "I think the most distressing thing was that you had the opportunity to tell me the day we were here at the cabin. But the photographs of Jeremy weren't on the mantel, were they? That's why you went inside ahead of me."

"I put them away."

"Why?" The pain of his deception was evident in her voice.

He looked up at the moon for a moment, then back at her. "I'm not sure. Partly because I didn't want you to feel sorry for me, to let your feelings about my loss color your feelings about, well, me."

"And the other part?"

"Because I didn't know at that point that you…that you couldn't have children." He raked a hand roughly through his hair. "I wasn't ready, didn't think you were ready, to talk about defective genes and CF matches. I didn't think either of us was ready so early in our relationship to discuss the implications of a potential match that could result in the birth of a child with CF."

Just like she'd felt it premature to discuss her childless state with him. "Probably not."

"I'm sorry."

"Me, too." She stared at him a long moment, searching his eyes. "I was mortified when your sisters told me about Jeremy. Not only because you hadn't chosen to share something with me that is so close to your heart, but because you'd allowed me to carry on about my childlessness and never said a word about what you'd suffered. It makes me feel ashamed."

"No, Abby, don't do that to yourself." He reached out to brush her arm. "I made an intentional decision not to tell you then because your pain was so fresh. You can't measure these things. Compare them. We've both been wounded deeply, borne a great loss, but in different ways."

She looked down at the ground.

"So," he ventured tentatively, "do you think you could reconsider staying in Canyon Springs?"

"No." She looked up at him again, her smile faint. "It wouldn't be wise."

"Why not?" He wanted to hear her say it. To say she didn't care for him. Didn't want any part of him.

"As I've said before, this is no longer my home. It would be awkward for us, don't you think, living our separate lives here in the same tiny town?"

She held out her hands for her keys, but he clenched them in his fist all the more tightly.

It was now or never.

"You're telling me you don't think there could ever come a time when you could return my love?"

With a soft gasp, Abby's eyes widened.

"Yeah, love, Abby," he whispered. "That's what I'm talking about. I'm coming to love you."

She had to stop him. No good could come of pursuing this line of thought. "Brett, we hardly—"

"Know each other? Then let's do something about that. Stay in Canyon Springs and let's spend time together."

"But—"

He gently gripped her arm, his gaze holding hers captive. "Tell me you don't care for me, too, Abby. I want to hear it."

How tempting it was to tell him she felt nothing for

him. It would be the right thing to do, to free him to marry someone who could give him children.

"Come on, Abby," his voice almost pleaded. "Tell me you don't care. If you can."

"You know it's not that easy. Especially not now."

"What do you mean?"

"Now that I know about Jeremy. Brett, you need the opportunity to be hugged on and loved on and your home filled with the rambunctious laughter of your kids. Your *biological* kids, half brothers and sisters to your precious son."

Brett's jaw hardened, the grief in his eyes apparent. She shouldn't have said that, shouldn't have reminded him of his little boy.

"I—we—can still have that, Abby. There's adoption, if you're open to it."

Her heart jolted. He loved her enough to give up having children of his own? "I can't ask you to make that sacrifice. God will lead you to someone else. You simply—"

"Pick some woman off the street who isn't a carrier of the defective gene like I am?"

A smile tugged at her lips. "Well, you could be a little discerning, Brett."

He shook his head. "Take it from me—love isn't a horse breeding operation where you study the bloodlines of sire and dam and make a suitable match for the most promising offspring."

"No, but—"

"Do you not *want* kids, Abby?"

She frowned. How could he ask her that, knowing the emotional and spiritual pain she'd endured? "I've always wanted children."

"Do you have anything against adoption?"

"No. But—" Her memory flashed to that fateful return flight from Los Angeles in December. "I've been told that any man who says adoption is an acceptable substitution to fathering his own offspring is a liar."

A stormy light sparked in Brett's eyes. "And who told you a stupid thing like that? That ex-fiancé who has no business parenting *any* child?"

"He said he had to be honest, and I respect that. He told me he could never love an adopted child like he could his own."

"Then I pity him." Brett's lip curled in disgust. "But I can tell you without a doubt that I can love an adopted child as much as any blood one."

She placed a hand on his arm. "How can you be sure, Brett?"

"Because that's another thing we haven't gotten around to discussing, Abby. *I'm* adopted." He waved a hand as if encompassing the world. "All of my siblings are adopted. And you know what? There's not one single day of my life that I haven't felt loved by my parents, by my whole family. I'm willing to confidently state that my siblings feel the same. So what do you say to that?"

She stared up at him. "Your folks adopted all seven of you?"

He quirked a smile. "Well, not all at the same time. But that's why I can assure you, Abby Diaz, that I'll be amazing beyond your wildest dreams with adopted kids."

She couldn't help but cringe. "Seven of them?"

"Could be." He winked. "What do you say we cross that bridge when we come to it?"

This was all happening so fast. So unexpectedly. "I don't know what to say."

"Then let me help you." He reached for her hand. "Repeat after me. 'Brett, my beloved—'"

"Wait, wait, wait." Her eyes narrowed in suspicion. Where was he going with this?

"You're the one who said you didn't know what to say.

I'm helping you out." He tugged at her hand to draw her close. "'Brett, my beloved, I believe with every ounce of my being that God put us on this planet at the same time and in the same place because He has a special plan for us. A plan to share our lives not only with God and each other but with kids who need a loving home. You're an amazing man, Brett Marden, and I love you with all my heart.'"

"I do love you, Brett." Joy filled her for an explosive moment, then doubt flickered. "But are you sure this is what you want? Never to have a blood-related brother or sister for Jeremy?"

"We both know there could never be another Jeremy. But loving and losing him opened my heart to all the possibilities God might have for me to bring happiness to another child who might otherwise never know God loves them."

"You *are* an amazing man."

"I know." He grinned. "I think, then, don't you, that we can now consider ourselves officially engaged? How about a trip next weekend to a Vegas wedding chapel?"

"Brett!" She punched him playfully in the arm.

He threw back his head and laughed. "I guess you have your heart set on a church wedding with family and friends underfoot."

"Don't you?"

He squinted one eye. "I have an awful lot of family, Abby. I don't think they'll all fit in Canyon Springs Christian. We might need to rent the high school gym."

"Or maybe the equine center arena," she suggested. "Since, you know, you'll be the assistant manager there."

He drew back. "Who told you that? That was supposed to be a surprise."

"You're not the only one who has an ear to the Canyon Springs grapevine, Mr. Marden."

"I guess not."

She glanced around the graveled Singing Rock parking lot, noting that half a dozen couples had come out on the lodge's porch to enjoy the moonlit evening. Then she tilted her head to playfully catch Brett's eye. "What do you say we give that grapevine something to talk about?"

He raised a brow. "Do you have something in particular in mind, ma'am?"

"As a matter of fact, I do. Happy birthday, cowboy."

And with that, she slipped her arms around his neck and drew him down for a kiss he'd never forget.

Epilogue

"Lookin' like a natural there, Abby!" cousin Olivia called from where she supervised a handful of boisterous children on the last day of the kids' camp. "With wedding bells on the horizon, it won't be long before you and Brett will be planning to have one of your own."

Abby winced, but managed a smile. *I don't understand why things had to be this way, Lord. I don't know that I'll ever understand. But I know You're in control and You love me and somehow You'll use my situation for my good and the good of others.*

She slipped her arm around the first-grader seated next to her on the picnic table bench, gave him a hug, then helped him glue the final pieces of a Popsicle-stick cabin he was constructing. Crafts, games, survival skills, nature walks and songs around a campfire. Boulder climbing and rappelling for those who were able and wanted to give it a try. Working with children on a daily basis all week had been both challenging and rewarding as she set aside her disappointments and endeavored to follow Brett's lead to love kids like Jesus would.

Let the little children come to me and do not hinder them...

Brett. What an amazing man God had blessed her with.

He said they weren't called to understand everything that happened in their life, but to trust God in the midst of it all, that the way to heal from pain was to reach out to others in theirs. She'd chosen to do that this week with children and parents who faced a lifetime of uncertainty, physical limitations and accompanying challenges.

"Would you two like more water?" Sharon Dixon, another camp volunteer, paused as she passed by with a stainless-steel pitcher of the cool liquid.

Both Abby and her little companion gratefully held out empty cups for a refill. The diamond engagement ring on Abby's finger glittered in the sunlight—as did the one on Sharon's hand. She and Dad had made it official and, like Brett and Abby, were planning a winter wedding. She'd heard City Councilman Jake Talford and Macy Colston had scheduled their nuptials for December, as well, Christmastime weddings seemingly becoming a Canyon Springs tradition. It was kind of a crazy one considering the unpredictable weather that time of year, but neither she nor Brett wanted to wait until spring.

"Thank you." Abby set her cup aside as Dad's fiancée turned away. "Sharon?"

The older woman paused, her kind eyes warming, and a thankfulness welled up in Abby that her father had at long last found someone to love who loved him in return.

"I want to say how happy I am for you and Dad. I mean that with all my heart."

"Thank you. I couldn't wish for a better stepdaughter. Your return to Canyon Springs has pleased your dad beyond measure, and your stepping into that school librarian position this coming autumn couldn't be better timed."

As Sharon continued on her way, Abby gazed around at her fellow volunteers, a number of them related to her in one way or another. She hadn't realized how much she'd missed extended family in those years after she'd been carted off to Tucson. Her mother hadn't missed the family, she knew that. Mom had never been close to hers and said more than once that there were too many Diazes underfoot in Canyon Springs. It had initially struck Abby the same way when she'd returned to town. All these people related by blood and marriage.

But it was growing on her quickly. She liked it. And it was a good thing, because Brett had a big family, too. When things wound down for the summer season, they'd be heading to the ranch where he'd grown up. She'd see Geri and Erin again and meet the rest of his family at an engagement celebration attended by, he'd reminded her, fifteen nieces and nephews. Plus Fergie. Mind-boggling.

She gave the little boy next to her another hug before he joined the other kids for one last walk through the woods. As he took off with a limping gait, a smiling Brett—for once not surrounded by a gaggle of giggling children—approached.

What was it about this handsome man in boots and a cowboy hat that set her heart racing?

"Howdy there, ma'am." Eyes twinkling, he settled in next to her at the picnic table, then leaned over to kiss her cheek. "It's been quite a week, hasn't it? Are you about ready to pack up these kids and send them home?"

"I'm tired, but I'm going to miss them." She looped her arm through his. "This has been hard work, but so much fun. I've gotten attached to so many and I can hardly wait to see them again next summer. Maybe we need to hold the camp *four* times a year. One week just isn't enough."

Brett laughed, the corners of his eyes crinkling. "You really did get into this, didn't you?"

"I did." Breathing in the scent of sun-warmed pine, she gazed happily at her surroundings, at the towering trees and the brilliant blue sky. The sound of giggling, chattering children filled her with an almost inexpressible sense of wonder. "This camp is amazing. I can see why you decided to get involved in it."

He took her hand, drawing her gaze back to him. "The doctor you found made it all possible. You know that, don't you? Thank you for making that effort even though it meant contacting your former fiancé's sister. She's been great. The kids love her and I think she's interested in joining us again."

"So it looks for sure as if there will be a camp next year?"

"And the year after that and the one after that and on down the road. Janet's brimming with ideas and is ready to sign a contract for the property for the next several years. This is an ideal location—cabins and other facilities that meet disability accessibility laws, space for pitching tents and all of it surrounded by rugged forest for the kids to get a genuine outdoor experience."

"Without being intimidated," Abby added, "by trying to keep up with kids who don't face the same physical challenges that they do."

"Exactly."

Still holding hands, they watched as children gathered in small groups around volunteers, preparing to head off on their last afternoon hike. It would be their final opportunity to test learned skills, to spot and identify woodland plants and animals. She'd learned a lot about the outdoors this week, too. In fact, the entire month in Canyon Springs had been a learning experience. Learning about herself and coming to a deeper understanding of God's love.

She gave a little sigh.

Brett glanced at her uncertainly.

She laughed. "What?"

"Is that a happy sigh or a sad sigh?" His words came softly as he squeezed her hand. "I heard what Olivia said to you about us having a baby. I know it hurts."

"That was a happy sigh, cowboy." She gave him a reassuring smile. "About the time we adopt the first of those seven kids, word will get around about our situation."

He grinned. "Like the news of having Jeremy in my life is already getting around. For so long I wasn't ready to share that part of me. But being able to openly talk about him feels right now. Already this past week I've encountered others who've suffered similar losses and need support."

"You honor your son's memory when you do that, Brett." Her gaze met his in mutual understanding. "I wish…wish I could have known Jeremy."

"You'd have loved him and he'd have loved you."

"And…" She lifted her hand to cradle the side of Brett's dear face. "I'd have loved to carry your child. Our child."

"I know, sweetheart." He slipped his arm around her and gently pulled her close. "God willing, though, we'll have a houseful of little ones God's handpicked. Kids who need a mom and a dad, who need to be loved as only we can love them."

Abby smiled at the thought. "We can do that. And if adoption doesn't work out, we can still make a difference in the lives of children through this camp and other opportunities."

"We can."

A ripple of joy bubbled up. "I love you, Brett. I'll never stop thanking God for bringing you into my life."

"I love you, too, Abby." He rested his head against hers.

"Brett?" A boy's voice broke into their solitude and they both looked up at Davy's friend Ace, who was standing a few feet away. He'd done well all week, no breathing problems, and his coloring looked healthy.

"What's up, bud?"

"You're going to go hiking with us, aren't you?"

Brett glanced at Abby. "I will if you'll let me bring this beautiful woman along with us."

Ace rolled his eyes. "Ohh…kay."

"Looks like I'm your man, then." With a clap of his hands, Brett rose. "Let's go."

"All right!"

Love in his eyes, Brett reached out to help Abby to her feet, and her heart swelled at the gift she'd been given.

"We're going to have a good life, Abby."

"We are."

He leaned down to give her a gentle, playful kiss. Then with a whoop, he tugged on her hand and together they jogged off after the laughing boy.

* * * * *

Dear Reader,

Brett's beloved son suffered from the genetic disease of cystic fibrosis, as do an estimated thirty thousand people in the United States alone. Hospitals in many states now test children for this disease at birth so that appropriate therapies can begin as early as possible. While treatments have vastly improved in recent years and longevity is increasing, there is no cure yet. Like my cousin Teri, many courageously await the hope of a lung transplant that doesn't come in time.

Sometimes, life hands us things that, quite frankly, we never "get over." There are things we'll never understand—realities that we live with for the whole of our lives, whether it be the loss of a loved one, a disability from birth, injury or illness, or the shattering of a dream. But that doesn't mean God has forgotten us. He can heal our hearts and bring us peace and hope even in the midst of our reality—if we choose to let Him.

That's what happens to Abby and Brett, who both suffered heart-crippling losses. Together they learn that gripping too tightly to the heartaches they've been dealt leads to scarring of the present and future, but choosing to trust God can empower them to live fully in the present and step courageously into tomorrow.

I love hearing from readers, so please contact me via email at glynna@glynnakaye.com or Love Inspired Books, 233 Broadway, Suite 1001, New York, NY 10279. Please visit my website at glynnakaye.com—and stop by loveinspiredauthors.com, seekerville.net and seekerville.blogspot.com!

Glynna

Questions for Discussion

1. Abby's parents not only divorced when she was young, but she was separated from her father and older brother from that point until the story opens. Why do you think the disappointments she recently suffered triggered a return to her hometown when previously nothing had?

2. Brett's suffered more than his share of devastating losses and when the door finally closed on a previous relationship, he was forced to move on and start over. Have you ever had a time in your life when doors closed with finality and you had to prayerfully reevaluate and begin anew?

3. Abby, too, has suffered a series of devastating disappointments. Do you sometimes feel able to handle a single situation or disappointment on your own, but when they come in multiples, it's a different story? How might Abby have been spiritually better prepared?

4. Brett blames himself for Melynda's departure and doubts he'd be a fit husband after his failure in that relationship. Do you think he's to blame for her abandonment, for her not coming to know the God he's come to rely on? How much responsibility can we take for the choices of others?

5. Abby returns to Canyon Springs with high expectations. Why do you think God may have allowed those expectations to be shattered almost immediately? Can

you understand why she initially wanted to turn her back on Canyon Springs again?

6. Brett immediately recognized a sadness in Abby. Have you ever met someone and right away sensed they'd suffered a deep loss even though they hadn't told you? What was it about your own life experiences that gave you the insight to recognize it?

7. In observing Abby and her father, Brett noted that divorce "did a number" on relationships that went far beyond the husband and wife. In what ways do you see that it affected Abby's choices, her relationships and her faith? How might her parents have better helped their daughter through their tragic breakup?

8. Except for his new friend Janet, Brett hadn't shared the loss that tore his world apart with anyone outside his immediate family. Why do you think this is? Why do you think he was able to share it with Janet and not others? How might that first step have prepared him for the arrival of Abby in his life?

9. Abby, too, is reluctant to share with her family the reason she and her fiancé broke up, telling herself she doesn't want to put a damper on the happy arrival of a new niece. What other reasons do you think she may have had for not wanting everyone to know of a loss that's broken her heart and crushed her dreams? Have you ever had something happen that's so deeply personal, so painful, that you weren't able to share it with anyone but God? Did there ever come a time when you were able to share it with others?

10. Brett's suffered deep wounds from what life has dealt him, yet he does his best to maintain a "life is good"

attitude and a sunny disposition. How much of that do you think is "personality" alone and how much of it is the result of his approaching life with a persevering, trusting and thankful heart?

11. Abby and her brother began renewing their childhood bond almost immediately, but the bond with her father was not so easily restored. Why do you think that was? Why do you think, even after such a long time, it came as such a surprise for Abby to discover her father was serious about a woman who wasn't her mother? What steps do you see both will need to take to continue to heal their relationship?

12. Abby and Brett are both refinishing furniture. Do you recognize the parallels that Brett sees in this process with the way God "refinishes" us and makes us fit to do the things He's placed us on earth to do? How do you think God may be working with you now to free you from the past and prepare you for the future?

13. Even though Abby still conversed with God, in many ways life's disappointments had sent her faith into hibernation. What evidence do you see of that? At what point do you see signs that her faith may be reawakening?

14. Considering their differences—city girl, country boy—what challenges do you foresee in the future for Brett and Abby? What "rough edges" do you think they'll need to turn to God to sand down and polish up?

15. Brett says you never "get over" tragedies and disappointments such as have impacted his life and Abby's,

but that God can and will heal over time as you grow closer to Him. Have there been things in your own life that you'll never "get over," yet God has brought comfort and peace in the midst of them? And if you've not found that comfort and peace yet, what steps do you need to take to draw closer to the God who loves you?

COMING NEXT MONTH FROM
Love Inspired®

Available April 15, 2014

HER UNLIKELY COWBOY
Cowboys of Sunrise Ranch
by Debra Clopton

Widow Suzie Kent needs help dealing with her troubled teenage son. Can tough sheriff Tucker McDermott prove he's the perfect man for the job?

JEDIDIAH'S BRIDE
Lancaster County Weddings
by Rebecca Kertz

When Jedidiah Lapp saves her brothers' lives, Sarah Mast quickly falls for the kind, strong hero. But when he must return to his own community, will they ever meet again?

NORTH COUNTRY MOM
Northern Lights
by Lois Richer

Alicia Featherstone never thought she'd have a family of her own. But she can see a future with former detective Jack Campbell and his adorable daughter...if she can make peace with her past.

LOVING THE LAWMAN
Kirkwood Lake
by Ruth Logan Herne

She vowed she'd never fall for another lawman, but when widow Gianna Costanza meets handsome deputy sheriff Seth Campbell, he could be the man she breaks her promise for.

THE FIREMAN FINDS A WIFE
Cedar Springs
by Felicia Mason

Summer Spencer knows it's risky to fall for a man with a dangerous job. But how can she resist falling for charming firefighter Cameron Jackson when he's melting her heart?

FOREVER HER HERO
by Belle Calhoune

Coast Guard hero Sawyer Trask has loved his childhood friend Ava for as long as he can remember. Will their second chance at love be destroyed by a painful secret?

_____

LOOK FOR THESE AND OTHER LOVE INSPIRED BOOKS WHEREVER BOOKS ARE SOLD, INCLUDING MOST BOOKSTORES, SUPERMARKETS, DISCOUNT STORES AND DRUGSTORES.

LICNM0414

REQUEST YOUR FREE BOOKS!

2 FREE INSPIRATIONAL NOVELS
PLUS 2
FREE
MYSTERY GIFTS

Love Inspired®

YES! Please send me 2 FREE Love Inspired® novels and my 2 FREE mystery gifts (gifts are worth about $10). After receiving them, if I don't wish to receive any more books, I can return the shipping statement marked "cancel." If I don't cancel, I will receive 6 brand-new novels every month and be billed just $4.74 per book in the U.S. or $5.24 per book in Canada. That's a saving of at least 21% off the cover price. It's quite a bargain! Shipping and handling is just 50¢ per book in the U.S. and 75¢ per book in Canada.* I understand that accepting the 2 free books and gifts places me under no obligation to buy anything. I can always return a shipment and cancel at any time. Even if I never buy another book, the two free books and gifts are mine to keep forever.   105/305 IDN F47Y

Name   (PLEASE PRINT)

Address   Apt. #

City   State/Prov.   Zip/Postal Code

Signature (if under 18, a parent or guardian must sign)

Mail to the Harlequin® Reader Service:
IN U.S.A.: P.O. Box 1867, Buffalo, NY 14240-1867
IN CANADA: P.O. Box 609, Fort Erie, Ontario L2A 5X3

**Are you a subscriber to Love Inspired books
and want to receive the larger-print edition?
Call 1-800-873-8635 or visit www.ReaderService.com.**

* Terms and prices subject to change without notice. Prices do not include applicable taxes. Sales tax applicable in N.Y. Canadian residents will be charged applicable taxes. Offer not valid in Quebec. This offer is limited to one order per household. Not valid for current subscribers to Love Inspired books. All orders subject to credit approval. Credit or debit balances in a customer's account(s) may be offset by any other outstanding balance owed by or to the customer. Please allow 4 to 6 weeks for delivery. Offer available while quantities last.

Your Privacy—The Harlequin® Reader Service is committed to protecting your privacy. Our Privacy Policy is available online at www.ReaderService.com or upon request from the Harlequin Reader Service.

We make a portion of our mailing list available to reputable third parties that offer products we believe may interest you. If you prefer that we not exchange your name with third parties, or if you wish to clarify or modify your communication preferences, please visit us at www.ReaderService.com/consumerchoice or write to us at Harlequin Reader Service Preference Service, P.O. Box 9062, Buffalo, NY 14269. Include your complete name and address.

LI13R

Love Inspired®

Hidden feelings, loving hearts

Sarah Mast gave Jedidiah Lapp a cherry pie and her heartfelt
thanks for saving her twin brothers from the path of a speeding
car. That should be that, but when she sees him again at Sunday
services, she realizes her heart is trying to tell her something
about the handsome man from Happiness, Lancaster County.
But when Sarah finds herself visiting Jed's community, he talks
about his future—and it's not at all what she expected. Is it all a
misunderstanding? Sarah is torn whether to hide her feelings.
She and Jed might have a chance at forever love, but only if
they're brave enough to speak from the heart....

Lancaster
COUNTY WEDDINGS

Jedidiah's Bride

by

Rebecca Kertz

Available April 2014 wherever
Love Inspired books and ebooks are sold.

LI87884